A MEMOIR OF JUNGLE JUNCTION

by Tim Kitson

faction Memoirs

Published by

OUTRIGHT FICTION

The Studio Oakleigh Parklands Road Bristol BS3 2JW UK

hello@outrightfiction.uk

Say hello to the author – tim@hiswritingplace.co.uk

ISBN 978-0-9571545-9-9

Cover Design by Leah Foster
leahfosterdesign@gmail.com

In love, one and one are one.

Jean Paul Sartre

After we have sold all of us to all of us, and the planet's unique resource has been exchanged for a world of unsustainable pelf, we will be given a new opportunity to ensure that each person contributes to and receives from society according to their ability and needs.

Nikolay Legachev

CONTENTS

Tim Kitson's Note

Me, You & the Others

Just to interrupt for a moment, before even we start, around the time of Vera de Vaal's loss, which you'll read about shortly, I took Roy Massey's advice and began keeping a diary. Roy said it could be a jokey record of my sweats as a journalist, but that also it would be a set of contemporaneous notes, always useful during those times in a court of law.

Well, I still have it – in fact, nowadays, them – twenty eight diaries in total.

Then, recently, drinking wine with Rosy around a crackling camp fire in the Limpopo Province bush, she and I talked of our early years as a sassy couple, and the fun we had in exposing skulduggery at high levels. The conversation persuaded me to write the story you're about to read.

I reinvigorated forgotten memories by reading my diaries. I also re-interviewed people that I had first interviewed years ago, effectively refreshing our joint recollections of past events, and that process – the revisiting of shared experiences, and the exchange of knowledge, detailed and often intimate – has enabled something special.

Obviously, I can write in the first person, about my personal involvement in this story, and I can talk with you directly in the second person, something Italo Calvino often enjoyed doing. Yet now, after hearing so many first-hand accounts anew, I can also offer a third person narrative, a memoir enabling me to tell you about the extraordinary contribution of the others to this tale.

With love and gratitude.

Thank you.

Tim Kitson
London
Spring 2024

Gazing Over the Southern Ocean

Woodstock

I started to recall things vividly a year ago, at the beginning of 2023. I was comfy and relaxed, sitting in the sunshine on the balcony of our small townhouse in the Woodstock area of Cape Town. There was a touch of sadness, Archbishop Desmond Tutu having died on Boxing Day over the Christmas period. Yet I was cheered by the local and online obituaries, the whole world had a need to shout-out about the anti-apartheid hero's 90-year spin on the planet. I read in one piece that Tutu was an exceptionalist, then I thought, hang on, there's no such word, though it described him perfectly.

That day on the balcony was a blue-sky affair, made snug by a soft berg-wind – a mass of desert air that had snailed its way south from the Karoo and enveloped Cape Town in a somnolent haze.

Along the nearby waterfront the tall dune grass moved quietly as the heat eased through it to move offshore, and halfway between the waterfront and our house was St Georges Cathedral, where the famous three-thousand-year-old cycadaceous palms were copying the dune grass, their ferny leaves fluttering quietly in the easy-going air, as if maybe waving Tutu goodbye.

Remarkably, that's exactly where he was, laying supine in a bright pine coffin, centre place in the nave of St George's, a few hundred metres from where I sat.

It said in one obituary that Tutu's wooden overcoat was the cheapest available and chosen by him personally – in fact, he actually ordered it, apparently. That would fit with his sense of self-effacement, although you can't believe everything you read in the newspapers, and I say that as a seasoned investigative journalist.

Across the coffin's unlacquered top a spray of white carnations lay still, radiating their prettiness with a diaphanous iridescence. One online pundit, a self-proclaimed Low Churcher, suggested the coffin might be a gesture of humility on Tutu's part, designed to help level the priestly authority of St George's. Yet most obituaries, including the one written by my old friend, Roy Massey, saw the coffin as a confirmation of Tutu's eco-friendly credentials, totally in keeping with his pre-death wishes of a no-frills funeral and an aquamation.

I hadn't heard of that, have you?

For those of you who don't know, an aquamation – alkaline hydrolysis is the proper name – is a flameless eco-friendly cremation. Tutu's body was to be immersed for a few hours in a solution of water and a powerful alkali, like, say, potassium hydroxide, inside a heated pressurised cylinder. The process would liquify all but his bones, which would be retrieved and kiln dried to a powder, before being placed in an urn and handed to the family.

What an amazing way to go!

Of course, it wasn't only in South Africa that Tutu was mourned – there were millions of admirers all around the world, and there were tightknit groups that loved him because he stood up for them, the LGBT communities, and the Palestinians, oppressed by their own form of apartheid which he was the first to recognise. I think the Palestinians saw Tutu as their saviour, a man of the church whose moral compass had a magnetic fix on the injustices of the West Bank. In outing the oppressive occupation of Palestine, Tutu exposed the most shocking irony of all – the apartheid policy adopted by the Israeli Knesset was developed by Hendrik Verwoerd, the architect of the South African policy of apartheid and separate development, who based his theory firmly on Nazi ideology.

∞

I met my journalist friend, Roy Massey, at the time the Truth and Reconciliation Committee began its work, chaired, of course, by Tutu. The archbishop's mantric words – *there can be no future without forgiveness* – provided the Truth and Reconciliation committee with an effective forcefield, a defence against those blacks who at the time were baying for white blood, uninterested in forgiveness – and because Tutu's words were ethically on the money, the whole world moved forward.

At the time there was no bigger news than the Truth Commission's revelations – the witnesses giving evidence, the truth commissioners listening, the confessors and the forgivers, the liars, and the committee cynics, they were all interviewed back-to-back in endless succession. As a senior reporter at The Cape Town Herald, Roy got to know Tutu, and other powerhouse brains such as Mandela and de Klerk, the Peace Prize Trio, together with other important contributors to the reconciliation process – people such as Andrew Mopeli and Joshua Chios.

As my boss, when I pitched up at the Herald as a new recruit, Roy took hold of me, steeping me in the arcane knowledge needed to survive as a rookie reporter. He compiled a starter-knows-fuck work roster that made certain I got to report on absolutely everything inconsequential. I covered fetes and wrote about five-year-old thwack the rat winners. Then there were the animals, cats stuck up trees, deceased hamsters, lots of them, and there was once a five-metre-long crocodile snoozing in The Royal Golf Club's carpark. Another time, I arrived in the Claremont suburb to find a huddle of sobbing women gathered over a huge dead python that had been shot in the head by a local policeman. Inside the snake's body, a metre or so from its mouth, was a large rugby ball-shaped bulge, ominously still. After a little questioning of the huddle, against a background of high-pitched communal wailing, I was able to confirm the rugby ball's identity as that of Vera de Vaal's poodle.

A couple of years after the poodle's demise, just prior to clearing my desk at the Herald to move on to the Johannesburg Post, there was Billy, a solitary, white pelican, inexplicably lost. I got the job, as a leaving joke, I think, of checking him out. The bird was enormous, an animated hang-glider, circling the city for hours each day, with its huge gular fishing sac slung slack beneath its gargantuan bill – I gave him the nickname, Billy, get it?

Billy's aerial splendour was a thingamajig of beauty. Metaphorically he obscured the ugliness of the apartheid era truths frothing beneath him. I asked the Herald's readers why Billy would have deserted the fellowship of his flock, and why he would have flown south for thousands of miles, alone? The subeditors reflexively deleted the anthropomorphic gush from my daily updates – nonetheless, I enjoyed penning the Billy column, and I particularly enjoyed speculating as to his motives. I could sense in Billy's gliding majesty, a lyricism. It somehow hinted at a better tomorrow – although at the time I had no idea that Billy would bizarrely end up saving my life.

Anyway, after a week of celebrity, Billy's sojourn in Cape Town ended and he set off, winging it north towards the border. I suppose there was a level of superimposed woe in my reporting when he departed. Rosy Lennox had also flown north, in her case two years earlier and to America on a one-way ticket. I understood Rosy's motives better than Billy's, she was leaving the racial squalor of South African society in defence of her own happiness. Yet still, I was puzzled at the ease of Rosy's leaving – she and I had shared a deep inseparability, or so I'd thought.

Sometimes, though, people just do things, don't they?

∞

I spent the whole of New Year's Day on the balcony. Tutu nipped off after his memorial service for the alkaline hydrolysis, but I stayed put in the sunshine – nut nibbling, wine glugging, and memory sifting.

The day's clear blue sky inspired a memory of Paul McCartney's concert in St Petersburg, in 2004 – it was pissing down beforehand, and then it became so bright the band's guitarist, Brian Ray, had to send for his sunglasses. It was no coincidence, either, that the skies were blue for the opening of the Beijing Olympics in 2008, or for the May Day celebrations in Moscow in 2016. On each occasion huge quantities of frozen carbon dioxide were dropped into the clouds to clear them. The technology, to both stop rain and to make rain, was developed in South Africa, but then it was weaponised, and it changed the world, as you'll discover.

Gazing out to sea during the late afternoon, a chimeric sphere of cheerfulness rose from the water around Robben Island. I imagined it was a bubble full of once-incarcerated innocents, untethered, floating free. Then, out of nowhere, I was right back in that moment of Mandela's long walk to freedom – the sun was shining, and Mandela was smiling, walking tall. The mood was palpable and very public – truth, reconciliation, and forgiveness were the qualities that would save us, and pave the way to a new South Africa.

Time moves on though, doesn't it? When Mandela left the table a few years back he was succeeded by Thabo Mbeki, a political squib who, after his hissing denial of AIDS, is remembered for thousands of unnecessary deaths. Mbeki now lives in a secure, electric-fence-razor-wire-protected cottage, with an armed response team on standby. Mbeki's home is in Riviera, a posh suburb of Jozi – local speak for Johannesburg – and it's in the area previously preferred by the racist, slave owning Randlords.

The next President was Jacob Zuma, who exchanged Mandela's vision of racial equality for the very different reality of State Capture, and made himself extraordinarily rich in the process.

∞

And now?

The current President of South Africa, Cyril Ramaphosa, once hailed as a reformer has transmogrified over the five years since he took office into a stoic reactionary, a partyman, a political blancmange with a constant wobble. Even so, he was invited as the first state-visit-guest of the UK's new King Charles III in the Spring of 2023, an overseas trip that offered him a welcomed break from the load-shedding-blackouts characterising his government's deficiencies back home.

The itinerary of a white-tie banquet at Buckingham Palace, and the opportunity to address the British Parliament and have a private chat and a cup of tea with Rishi Sunak, the Prime Minister, created a unique experience not only for Ramaphosa but also for the British Royal Family – Ramaphosa being the only guest of the British Monarchy ever to have had several million dollars in cash found stashed down the back of his sofa, the proceeds from the sale of animals, apparently – cash cows, maybe?

Prior to packing his white-tie, Ramaphosa came under renewed pressure at home with loud criticism of his government's running costs, and of its perceived rock and roll life style. Most ordinary black South Africans have dovetailed their existence to fit the scheduled daily blackouts, midst record rates of unemployment, street violence and a deepening sense of inequality. However,

Ramaphosa's ministers party each night in their purpose built 265-acre, leafy and fortified compound, kept out of the dark with portable generators. To make commuting easy there's a helipad, and for leisure time there's a golf course, plus an array of tennis courts and a health spa.

∞

My balcony-day drew to a close with a stunning vista – the sun was sinking and flaming, with the Southern Ocean rising to claim it – a magical few moments that reminded me of the insoluble miracle of creation. How did time and space appear from nothing, from such absolute nothingness? Could a similar miracle embrace our Rainbow Nation? After all, hope springs eternal, doesn't it? According to the Greek poet Theognis, hope is the only good god remaining among humankind. Maybe, but as the sun was taken under I sensed a veil, nothing more than a gossamer filament, yet it smudged my outlook – the harvest had ended, the summer had gone, and we were not saved – there was no new South Africa.

Moses Kimbo

Jozi

All those years ago, on the morning that Billy the pelican set off from Cape Town, winging it north towards the border and Mozambique, possessed of the visual sharpness for which a pelican's sight is renown, he would have seen below him an old-fashioned racist. A spent and half bent man, shambling towards parliament's colonnaded entrance on his way to a trade-off – in exchange for his cooperation there would be a guarantee of immunity from prosecution.

I also flew north that morning, to Easthope in the lowveld, to a wedding and a reacquaintance after two years with Rosy Lennox, who would be there as her sister Emma's maid of honour. Also, at around six that morning, a few hours before Billy and I got started, and a thousand miles from Cape Town in Jozi, Jabulani Kimbo climbed into the passenger side of his brother's lorry cab and slammed shut the door, ready for a short ride to work.

∞

"What's this news junk you got on the radio, man? You's a truck driver, play some music."

Moses, relaxed in the driver's seat, his ridged forearms lying slack across the Volvo's outsized steering wheel, registered his younger brother with two bloodshot yet attentive eyes, nestled below a furrowed brow and a thin canopy of salt and pepper curls that were jigging.

"Listen up, Jabu," Moses said. "You know those white bastards killed our cousin Nancy, and they never said so before 'cos they'd a been walking air on the end of a rope? Well, now they're gonna tell us what they did so they can walk away from it all with this amnesty shit."

"Moses, we both know they should be fucked, man."

"Yeah. It's the way they did our Nancy, keeping her naked in that hole for weeks, plastic carrier bag fashioned into a pair of panties. Shooting her in the back of the head, while she's snuggled up foetal like, like a little one."

"What didn't they do? They held us for months

without reason." Jabu said.

"Yeah, that was nothing – they stole from us, poisoned us, bombed us, threw us out of aeroplanes."

Moses warmed to the joke of it all and was smiling, flashing a collection of gaps between his surviving teeth.

"Pushed us through sixth floor windows." Jabu said.

"Hung us in our prison cells."

"Blew us to bits in our cars. Moses, hang a left here and drop me on the corner. I need some smokes."

"It ain't right, these people walking."

"Moses, what about us, what we did? We gonna walk any air?"

"Shit, Jabu, we did freedom fighting, self-defence."

"Moses, forget this stuff, yeah? I mean, what are we gonna do about it? Tell me about our new truck, my new truck. How is it?"

"It's still on. A few thousand more and it's in the bag.'

"You's being saying that a while now, Moses."

"Little brother, you sure you wanna put that saxophone away and be a trucker?"

"Stop playing? No man, I just need money. I ain't Jabu Masekela, I'm Jabu ain't-got-fuck Kimbo. Buy me that truck, brother. Moses, you ain't got a bad voice. That band we had was really cooking, and you've got a fit-looking body. You's always pumping iron, but get your teeth fixed. You can't sing for money with a mouth like that."

Moses winked a thankyou and began braking towards the corner.

"When am I seeing you?"

"Back Tuesday." Moses said.

"OK, brother."

∞

Jabu stepped down from the cab's stainless-steel runners and Moses nosed Constance away to find his route out of Jozi – Moses had named the Volvo in honour of his late mother. Packed in the back of Constance were assorted wood carvings, thousands of them – animals, plates, letter openers, souvenirs for the tourist trade. Moses was at the start of an eleven-hour journey towards the Outeniquas

Mountains, and their famously high and narrow pass, before rolling on down the hills on the far side towards Mossel Bay and the jade-coloured shallows of the Indian Ocean.

∞

There had been a period when Moses committed to the ANC and the armed struggle – he had travelled secretly to Ethiopia for training, before spending a couple of years hitting South African government installations from Angola. Now though he was settled and happy, running his own small business and, as far as he could, forgetting the past.

Moses began with a fourth-hand, clapped-out motorbike, delivering small parcels and documents, but progressed to his present pride and joy, the fourteen-metre Volvo that purred sweetly as he motored south that morning.

With the radio still tuned to Talk 24 he listened to the studio team berate the black government's lack of success. The reconstruction programme had failed. The economy was on its knees. There was a skyrocketing, drugs-driven crime rate.

Unlike his namesake, Moses didn't know how he and his black brothers would be delivered from the wilderness. There had been talk, a lot of it, but no burning bushes. In the Hillbrow suburb where Moses and Juba lived, expectations were still rising but the promise of new homes and schools was unfulfilled. The way Moses saw it, black politicians were sucking up to the very people responsible for the mess, and when the station's studio team revisited the amnesty process, suggesting that some whites should be held to account and not pardoned, Moses bellowed at the radio as if it were sentient.

"YES, those bastards who killed our Nancy. And Cyril's boys, ruined the man's life. All he's ever seen is a photograph, two of 'em lying rigid, a bullet between the eyes, and Jesus, their hearts!"

∞

By nine that morning Moses had been driving for three hours, and Cape Town had begun to ooze a claggy warmth. Benzened air lay as set jelly across the scorched, salt-flat ghettos, and downtown that old-fashioned racist had reached Parliament's colonnaded entrance. At the lobby's revolving doors he paused for breath, wondering why it had been necessary for him to rest, and for a moment he watched an enormous white pelican fly overhead.

After flashing a pass at the entrance attendant he moved on through security and walked the length of the banqueting hall, before turning right into the caucus and committee room corridors, eventually arriving at the suite of offices that accommodated the Ethics Committee. Hung along the corridor walls, among a large collection of photographs, was one that featured our old-fashioned racist, General Daniel Jackson, Chief of the Reconnaissance Commandos (the Recces) known by all as Jacko's boys. The general's portrait was alongside other top brass from the military and a full house of ex-presidents and Prime Ministers, stretching forward from the Act of Union in 1910, with the assassinated architect of Apartheid, Hendrik Verwoerd, hanging a few frames to the right of his own. Verwoerd once described apartheid as a policy of good neighbourliness – strange way to talk about the systemic racial segregation that he enforced.

That Old-fashioned Racist

Cape Town

Jacko was anxious and adrenalised, a combination that produced the jitters, and he was about to bluff a parliamentary subcommittee. If it worked a negotiated immunity would provide a clean slate on which he could doodle away his retirement years, supported by a fortune in crisp $100 bills of which the subcommittee knew nothing. In any event, either he testified, or he faced the prospect of the subcommittee unravelling twenty years of his private life, in public – they were about to hang out South Africa's dirty washing for the world to inspect. Jacko could see no point in reconstructing the past, pointing the finger, exhuming the bodies. The majority of Jacko's white racist friends were unconvinced they had played a role in apartheid's social abuse – they mostly thought apartheid was a good idea, just badly executed.

Jacko took a seat, surrounded by a circle of support staff, and surprised at Andrew Mopeli's absence, having expected him to be there with a quiver of pointed and poisoned questions. In fact, Andrew, like me, was on his way to the wedding at Easthope. So, in Andrew's place, staring directly at Jacko was Joshua Chios, one of the black Government's brightest young lawyers. Chios had greyed prematurely and in contrast to his skin tone there was a conspicuous, thin-cut white moustache, often smoothed and flattened by his index finger and thumb.

"General, what decision have you come to?" Chios said.

Jacko was immediately disturbed by the lawyer's elegance, another gauche example of new-age impertinence. An expensive suit was addressing him, French or Italian, and a silk tie hung loosely from Chios' sharp, white cotton collar, and the shirt's overlong sleeves were clasped with gem-encrusted cufflinks. Jacko spotted a Rolex similar to his own, dangling loose from the lawyer's wrist.

"Did you hear my question?" Chios said.

"Yes. I'll co-operate. Immunity from prosecution in

return for what I know about the Recce ops in Mozambique and Angola, and I'll give evidence under oath."

"I assume in what you know, will be information as to how the Recces were funded, what atrocities were committed and who was responsible?"

Apparently, Jacko knew they had him by the balls, and so agreed, readily.

"Good. In your last interview you were asked to consider whether there were other issues you should let us know about. What else is there?"

"Nothing at the moment. I intend to give you names, of the people who moved from the military to organised crime, but it's better done in the context of my witness statement."

"Better holding off until after we've granted immunity? Hum? General Corby, you had a question?" Chios said.

"Yes, thank you. Jacko, I'm told there's a report, commissioned by de Klerk, limited edition, and you have a copy."

"Colby, I've been in possession of various sensitive reports, but these days they will be found in the archives for which you, as my successor, are now responsible."

"General, what can you tell us about your involvement in the death of President Machel of Mozambique?" Chios said.

"Not much, other than wishing the bastard dead long ago. We all know he was killed in a plane crash, more than that I can't say."

"Thank you, General. We'll be in touch."

Chios stood to leave, pocketing his pen in the deep silk interior of his suit jacket, revealing a powerful, lean physique – Chios was young, fit, successful, and intellectually strong, not that Jacko could ever have seen a black creature in that way.

Colby bided his time, slowly shuffling things.

"Jacko. if these people catch you out, you're fucked, you know that, don't you? They'll withdraw the offer of immunity and prosecute you."

"Colby, the best way you can help me right now is to get me out of this fucking chair. My legs have seized up. My whole body's asleep. As for the other stuff, thanks for the advice but I know what I'm doing. I have the low-down, more than enough to keep pretty-boy Chios happy."

Colby offered an arm, and Jacko's circulation pulsed back when he stood upright.

"Not everyone is in favour of amnesty. If Chios prosecutes you, it won't be a gentle affair."

"Colby, you couldn't stand the pain of knowing half what I know. If you ever discover what this country has been up to for the last twenty years it's going to feel a bit like having a corn-cob wrapped in razor wire thrust up your lily-white liberal arse."

∞

Emerging from the engineered coolness of the ethics committee offices, Jacko strode off laboriously through the pedestrian precinct with a deepening sense of physical sufferance. In front of the library he crossed to Concordia Street and walked towards the impressive stained-glass windows of St Mary's Church. The Church's reinstated portico – the messaging of the original was too pagan according to the Victorian Boers who removed it – frames an always-open dark oak door and a chandlery, where Jacko paused to collect a candle and slide a coin through the wooden alms box slot. The Friends of St Mary's had hung a plaque on the new portico wall, but Jacko managed only a paragraph before stomping off into St Mary's semi-darkness with a feeling of contempt for its elegiac content.

> 'The Boers demolished St Mary's original portico, together with its praiseworthy history of the San People, while applying white supremacist notions of evolution to the human race. Publication of 'The Divine Hierarchy of Being' led the Boers to mistakenly believe that they were at the top of the evolutionary scale.'

Jacko placed his candle with others already flickering a dappled pattern across the buff-coloured stone of the transept wall. He took a seat, closed his eyes and prayed, and never having experienced a tension between his faith, the racist realities of apartheid and his murderous personal responsibility of commanding the Recces, he did so with a feeling of admittance and ease.

Jacko opened his eyes to see the Dean standing a few metres to his left in the aisle.

"General, welcome to St Mary's. I'm sure if Andrew Mopeli were to see you in the church from which he has given so many no-nonsense readings, it would bolster his belief in miracles."

"And possibly his propensity for forgiveness, given that's what he intends to have done with me, Dean, to forgive me."

Jacko was feeling even stiffer, his legs were ponderous. Pulling himself upright from the pews was a drawn out affair, ending with him stepping clumsily in to the aisle.

"Can I be of assistance?"

"Thank you. Dean, I realise you may be surprised to see me in St Mary's, but I feel God's embrace here, as I would in any church."

"General, do you want to be forgiven?"

"Not especially, but it comes with immunity from prosecution."

"So you don't regret what you did?"

"Regret?"

"A lot of people died."

"Dean, you don't count the dead when God's on your side. I helped protect this country, firstly from communism and secondly from a black insurrection that would have flushed South Africa down the pan overnight. Now communism is no longer a force in the world, people forget how threatening it was to be surrounded by machete wielding maniacs hell bent on slaughtering us in our beds. My Recces had to combat a total onslaught from gorilla insurgents, and I mean gorilla, as in ape, tens of thousands of the black bastards, armed with first world weapons, paid for by Russia and Cuba and China.

"And as for black insurrection, the way the present Government is running the show, aided and abetted I may say by Andrew Mopeli and yourself, it may still succeed in inciting such an event."

∞

Jacko left St Mary's and crossed the newly renamed Mandela Avenue towards Chequers Bank, where he asked for the manager.

"Nice to see you Larry."

"You too, Jacko. How is it?"

"Not bad, but I'm a bit under the weather today, slow, and I've spent the last hour having my balls crushed by an elitist black."

"Sounds painful. Let's go down to the vaults, follow me. There's a rumour circulating, says you're about to resign. Is it true?"

"It's not a rumour, it's fact. Mopeli has forced my resignation as part of an immunity deal."

"Jesus, end of an era." Larry said.

Three floors below road level they approached a brightly lit, deposit-box vault, its door flanked by two armed guards.

Larry waited outside the vault, as always. He stood contemplating the new political order, which in many ways he saw as a new-fangled moral order. A black majority government had arrived with a new mandate – it was a frightening prospect, definitely time to wind things up.

Larry was surprised on Jacko's return to be handed both deposit box keys.

"I don't have need of the box any longer."

∞

Jacko shouted ring home at his mobile and in a moment Muriel was there.

"Hi, darling. How is it?"

"It's going fine."

"You agreed to testify?"

"Yeah. They're after more info but the deal's there. I'm just leaving the bank – two hours or so to Mossel Bay and forty minutes to the gorge, so I'll see you around three."

"Okay, darling. Drive carefully."

Jacko had the look of exactly what he was, an aged and self-indulgent racist soldier. His paunch smothered the buckle of his handmade belt and rippled each time his Mercedes clipped a pothole, and his neck, but hard to say how, was wider than his ears. His drooping jowls had lost the battle with gravity years back, although over time they had somehow synchronised themselves to slink in time with the rippling paunch. Jacko's eyes were puffy half-moons, the colour of coffee, and after sixty-two years under the African sun his face was a blotchy constellation of moles. The glittering collection of gold in his teeth underlined a notion of excess, although the nuggets were a wonder to see each time his wizened lips parted to expose them.

Like most of his generation, Jacko wore just-below-the-knee length shorts that ended a few inches above long thick woollen boy-scout socks, and that afternoon his shirtsleeves were crumpled to the elbow. Jacko's wrists and hands glittered like the bullion in his mouth but with the gold of jewellery and the chrome of a manacle, from which a chain angled off left towards the front passenger seat and the attaché case retrieved from the bank vault.

Jacko was in good spirits but still feeling slow. Even with air swirling about his open-topped car he felt tired, and fidgety, continually reseating himself in an effort to stay sharp. As a distraction he clicked the radio on and found a news channel. To his surprise, he was the news.

"General Jackson, whose surprise retirement has been announced, was instrumental in the sacking of dissident defence staff and their replacement with individuals sympathetic to the Government's intention to modernise the country's defence system, with the purchase of light utility helicopters and advanced light fighter aircraft. General Jackson was personally responsible for the procurement process, which has been mired in controversy since the trial and subsequent imprisonment of the European aircraft manufacturer's sales director on charges of corruption."

In his peripheral vision Jacko followed the dangling chromium chain from his wrist to the passenger's seat, and exposed the bullion in his mouth with a wide smile, in the knowledge of the attaché case's contents.

Shug's arrival, and The San

Easthope

In 1891 the plains of Camdeboo were as inhospitable to Shug Lennox as they had been thousands of years earlier to the San People, the aboriginal hunter gathers of the Southern African plains. Incredibly, the origin of our modern scientific thinking lay in the San's ancient way of hunting across the Camdeboo – their skills produced a willingness in them to continually modify their view of the world. When new evidence came to light from hunting experiences they would adapt their approach to accommodate the new knowledge – nowadays, that analytical technique is called the hypothetico-deductive method.

It's even taken a hold with me, researching this story, mixing new facts with existing knowledge. Take the mystery of San rock art – miniature, and exquisite – paintings produced in a period of pre-history before the written word, enabling abstract ideas and mental experiences to be seeable, yes, readable, before the written word. The San people have the world's oldest DNA, and in the same way that early human life is no longer thought of as nasty, or unknowing, then no longer should the San people be thought of as primitive, or stupid – a concept the East India Company settlers and the Afrikaners, and the proselytising authors of The Divine Hierarchy of Being, just didn't get, ever.

∞

Shug crossed the untamed wilderness of the Camdeboo on horseback, thirty-eight days of near isolation as he rode from Cape Town to Easthope, where he bought a plot and began farming, and where years later I would attend his great-granddaughter's marriage to Stefan Taylor.

The wedding was in the open air, under a wide African sky and beneath the canopy of an aged jacaranda tree, a self-assured specimen that rose to over fifty feet in the grounds of the family chapel. Magically, for the duration of a ceremony spanning more than an hour, the jacaranda's pale purple petals cradled themselves downwards onto the guest's heads and their assorted millinery, before fluttering to the ground to accumulate over the tough, spiky grass as a nuptial carpet. The organic confetti unfocused the gathering, and ethnicity and colour were washed together in the light, purple snowfall.

Some guests shook the petals free, others welcomed their arrival. Jordan Atwell, famous around Easthope for his mendacity and inestimable fortune, shook each foot alternately, irritated by the floral coverage of his brogues patina. Two rows behind Atwell and one ahead of me was Dorothy Tutani MP – she not only allowed the petals to settle but occasionally looked down to consider their charm. Dorothy spent most of her week in the Parliament Buildings from which Joshua Chios was at that moment staring blankly from a first-floor window in contemplation.

The vicar seated us for Andrew Mopeli's reading from Ecclesiastes, which was delivered with a diction gifted from Sussex University, where he spent four years completing a seminal PhD on Ubuntu. After twenty-two verses he closed the Old Testament bible and recited the final lines from memory.

"To everything there is a season, and a time to every purpose under Heaven. A time to be born and a time to die, a time to break down and a time to build up."

Dorothy Tutani turned to talk with her husband.

"Finnius, why don't you speak like that, and why aren't you six-and-a-half foot tall with the looks of Shaka, our great Zulu leader. Come to think of it, your complexion, it doesn't have that same quality of polished marble that Andrew's has."

"No, but I've promised to stay sober and drive you home, so behave yourself."

Dorothy heard me giggle and turned.

"Hi Tim, Andrew looks fantastic, doesn't he?"

"I wonder if he'll ever remarry." I said.

"Took him a long time to come to terms with Portia's death. He couldn't accept she was actually on

Samora Machel's plane when it crashed."

∞

After a final prayer of thanks, Emma and Stefan led us from the shade of the purple jacaranda through a red corridor of flamboyance trees hanging in breathtaking full-bloom vermilion. We emerged into a few metres of bright sunshine before entering the starched white order of an impressive marquee, where we breathed life into the enormous canvas lung with an endless chin-wagging and a vibrant bonhomie, jabbering together in circles – three hundred of us spread over thirty round tables, stunningly festooned with tall wild-grown arum lilies.

Andrew, Dorothy, Rosy, and I had been seated together and were adjacent the head table, where the best man Theo Mason was over busy with his speech notes.

"Dorothy, how are things here." Rosy said.

"As a member of the Government it's my duty to tell you we have a lovely climate and a wonderful country. No better place to be. We have a new liberal constitution, commissions to safeguard gender and human rights, and a black Government with a social conscience."

"Sounds pretty good."

"Rosy, between you and me, the country's in a mess." Dorothy said.

"But on the plus side, we now have a very colourful new flag." I said.

"Yet everything's a problem, you name it – policy implementation, expenditure on education, new-build housing, tourniqueted to a drip, and criminal gangs hold sway over the urban landscape." Andrew said.

"In Jozi they shoot motorists on a daily basis, just to hijack a vehicle for a heist." Dorothy said.

"One young mother had her white brains blown out as she sat with her children at traffic lights, part way through the school run." Andrew said.

"Oh my God."

"And Rosy, wandering in no man's land, mostly black, mostly poor, are ten million men, women and children, with AIDS." Dorothy said.

"This all sounds dreadful. What's the score with AIDS?"

"It's a price issue, Rosy. People can't afford

antiretroviral drugs, Vuka Kwabifile they call them – wake up from dying." I said.

"And housing, the backlog is three million. Rosy, we don't have the money or the skills to change much, and the people's patience is running on empty. I've decided to head up the Azanian Housing Cooperative, it's a not-for-profit newbuild outfit, but we need money." Dorothy said.

"If nothing happens the land issue will be back, people are pissed, they'll start tearing down fences, and the future, it'll be lost in the dust." Andrew said.

"I read you're a prominent figure in public life these days, Andrew. The driving force behind the Government's Ethics Committee." Rosy said.

"The journalist must have been a friend of mine."

"Maybe, the article mentioned your work in exile, and that you'd been invited back to teach the politics of Ubuntu."

"We can't go forward until we create a climate of openness. People need to come to terms with the past on a morally acceptable basis. Obviously, the victims and their families can't forgive what happened until they know what happened. So, in the tradition of Ubuntu – *umuntu ngumuntu ngabanye bantu* – the wrong-doers and the wronged, they have to become better people through each other."

∞

After the speeches and toasts Andrew Mopeli caught up with the world, walking several circuits of an unimpeachably flat croquet lawn, listening to a batch of voicemails, one of which required a ring-back and so he returned Joshua Chios' call.

"Andrew, General Jackson's a bastard." Chios said.

"Joshua, you are not seconded to me to fuck these people. Your job is to advise on the correct legal context of their applications for immunity. If they don't co-operate, fine, they're yours. If they do co-operate, they're walking free, forgiven."

"Calm down, Andrew. How's the wedding?"

"Delightful. What did he have to say?"

"He'll co-operate, and under oath. He's says he'll spill the beans and give us names, but only after immunity is agreed and he's in the clear. At the same time he's denying involvement in actions we know he took part – like the assassination of Samora Machel. He also denied having a copy of the de Klerk report."

"Okay, Joshua, stay on it."

Re-entering the tent Andrew strolled towards the head table, intent on congratulating the newlyweds a second time. He waved hello to me on the way past and nodded to Jordan Atwell as he passed him.

Atwell seemed preoccupied with events elsewhere, squinting at a text and side-tracked further by the stubbornness of a last jacaranda petal lodged between the lace and the tongue of his left brogue.

Andrew kissed Emma on the cheek and hugged her, and then he shook Stefan's hand, beaming a well-done-hope-you'll-be-happy smile.

"You both look fabulous, you really do. Hey, Stefan, that Recce operation, that Theo mentioned in his speech, saving his life when you were in the army together, where was that?"

"A small village called Kassinga, middle of Angola."

"Sounded scary."

"Yeah, it wasn't a breeze."

"Stefan, you know what I do for a living at the moment. If you ever need to talk, come see me."

"Thanks, Andrew, I'll keep it in mind."

"OK, have a great honeymoon. I'm off to have a chat with Tim.

∞

"Stefan?"

"Sorry, Emma, miles away, Andrew got me thinking, Kassinga, it was hell."

"I know it was, you've said, but never how. Andrew's invitation, it could be a positive experience to talk with the Ethics Committee. Why don't you start by talking to me, tell me what happened in Angola."

"Okay, but not today. Ironic, isn't it? All that Angolan shit. I was so traumatised the army took me off ops and seconded me to Rainmaker, and we met. I pitched up at the farm with Gillmor to do a six-month stint. Ah, well, you would remember that, 'cos following my reassignment he stayed on and you got the hots for him."

"What a thing to say on our wedding day! True

though, but a big mistake, he was never my sort."

"That's not what he thought."

"Stefan, we have a plane to catch, because I didn't marry Gillmor, I married you, and we're off on honeymoon."

∞

"How's the world of journalism?"

"Busy as ever, Andrew, what with all the truth you're exposing at the Ethics Committee hearings."

"Well, keep up, Tim. We need the coverage, but you'll need to swim through shit to reach the real truth." Andrew said.

"That is it! Isn't it? Political shit, black and white, military shit, black on black racist shit, white supremacist shit. How about Ethics Committee shit, any of that about?"

"A little, but we tend to dig deep holes and bury it, so as not to attract predators, especially those who think the pen mightier than the sword."

"Me? How's it going?"

"There's still opposition within some ANC circles, but nothing will affect completion of the amnesty process. That's probably all I should say. You're mostly broadsheet, but you've been known to tabloidize the odd exclusive."

"Andrew, everything's off the record. You've given me such amazing stuff in the past I wouldn't use anything without permission."

"Alright, good of you to say."

"So?"

"You can't use it. I need a signed witness statement first. I just talked with Chios, looks like Jacko will testify."

"Christ! Talk about shit, I doubt there's a fan big enough for what he knows. I can see why there's still opposition from some of the ANC about what you're doing. It's incredible you intend to let Jacko walk free, the man's killed thousands."

"I know what he did, but you can't take revenge on a million whites, not unless you're into genocide as a pastime. We need to forgive, it's the only way forward. Hey, have you unearthed anything more on the report that de Klerk commissioned? Joshua says Jacko is denying its existence."

"No, but Hilton Clarke is launching a book on the

de Klerk years. I’m interviewing him on Monday for an editorial-cum-publicity piece. In fact, I’ve read the book and pre-written the article, simply need a few live quotes. Clarke would have been privy to such things. If I can slide him into a journalistic corner, you know, present him with an invidious choice, admitting the report’s existence or, alternatively, lying on the record to deny it, he may confirm its existence."

"I'll get a copy of Monday's Herald."

"Well, no. I've just started at the Johannesburg Post, working with Bruce Pontin – so, get a copy of Monday's Post.

Distance Poisoning

The Outeniqua Mountains

Moses slipped Constance down a gear and let her scream. Just a few miles from the final downhill he was conjuring the taste of a cold beer while negotiating the last of the mountain's switchbacks and hairpins – tight, blind pulls to the left and right. The last twist of the pass opens out onto the Gourits Bridge, a dizzy 120 metres above its eponymous river, before the road runs relentlessly downwards to sea level and the Indian Ocean.

∞

Thirty minutes earlier, coming in the opposite direction, in a layby just prior to the foothills, Jacko had been unnerved to find himself in a dazed state, leaning against the bonnet of his parked Mercedes. Refastening the chrome security cuff to his wrist came with a realisation that part of the day had disappeared, and where was his shirt? After a few moments collecting himself he decided to drive on, yet struggling to recall what had happened. Jacko passed the Lazaretto Cemetery blowing a kiss in the direction of his mother's grave, before turning right and passing the yacht club along the Santos Beach Road. The Mercedes climbed on the easy gradient through two thousand feet, and the mountain air began to restore Jacko's perceptions, although the float of his foot over the accelerator and brake had lost its lightness. A few miles on he reached the intermediate plateau at the start of an eight-mile straight that lead through an expanse of fynbos, with its small heather-like trees and shrubs, towards the distant but visible Gourits Bridge and home.

Jacko peered in the direction of the dashboard and shouted at his mobile to ring home, yet there was nothing for the voice recognition software to hear, just a wet, rasping wheeze. He tried again, but the same wordless effort brought silence a second time, and with it the knowledge for Jacko that he was partially paralysed. Then, slumping to his right with the door's armrest taking his almost-dead weight, a movement in the wing mirror caught his attention – he saw the buzzing in his ears, a helicopter, impudently close, so close the pilot must have sensed it was all over.

In Jacko's memory a sketchy recognition of the past took shape. It coalesced with the present and a precarious reality emerged, allowing Jacko to understand the enormity of what was happening to him. He recognised the previous impulse to discard his shirt, and he recognised his shallow breathing as the penultimate phase of a hands-off murder, a distance poisoning.

Jacko slowed the Mercedes to a stop on the far side of the bridge, only a few hundred metres from his home, but he could go no further. In his confused state he cut the engine without parking the gear lever. When his foot eased off the brake the vehicle moved hesitantly backwards, falling off the tarmac into an inadequate dirt margin on the far side of the road, and was held motionless between a safety barrier and a small outcrop of rock. A smaller car would have scurried through, plunging to the swirling rapids below, yet the Mercedes had a bumper width that held Jacko tenuously on the right side of the afterlife.

He opened the car door and fell into the dirt, in the sure knowledge he had been zapped with a nerve agent. He could remember the covert briefings on distance poisoning, and the technique of saturating a victim’s clothing and belongings with deadly toxins. He could even remember some of the early casualty's names and the way of their ends, such as the dissident policeman that he had murdered – who died only after six hours of paralysed agony, as he watched his own body transmogrify into a ball of boiling pus – organic magma slithered from beneath his sloughed skin and glugged its way to the floor.

Jacko gradually garnered his thoughts. Pulling himself upright he retrieved the attaché-case keys from his pocket and managed to unlock the cuff from his wrist, an essential precursor to stripping, which he knew was essential. But then he faltered and fell sideways, slumping involuntarily across the car’s front wing, pushing the attaché case over the radiator grill to the ground, from where it bounced obliquely into the road.

He began again, negotiating his belt buckle and dropping his shorts, removing his shoes, and tackling his underwear. He took off his watch and removed three gold rings from his podgy fingers, hungry for air. Lastly, a silver St Christopher, a present from his mother he had worn every day since his sixteenth birthday, slid between his exposed pectorals and downwards over his bare paunch to the ground.

A few moments later he was able to lean over the driver's door, pink and trembling, heavy and breathless, and turn the ignition.

"Ring home."

It was a croaky command, but stripped of the nerve agent it worked. After a few moments Jacko heard Muriel's voice and interrupted her with a slow squawking wheeze.

"Muriel, I'm ill. Come and get me, our side of the bridge."

Then Jacko fell across the car's bonnet a second time, immobile and exhausted, near to death, yet alive.

Within seconds, Muriel raced from their home.

The high-pitched sound of a lorry engine reached a crescendo as she bounded towards the road, and a large Volvo truck passed in front of her. Out of the corner of his eye Moses glimpsed the blurred legs of a white woman, thrashing beneath the held-high hem of a rose-patterned summer dress.

Moses emerged from the last blind hairpin and saw the Mercedes, directly ahead, on his side of the road. With Constance bent tight his first impulse was to hit the horn and not the brakes, if he locked her up that would be the end of everything. Even so, he hit the brakes and began pumping – foot on, foot off, to avoid a skid – and he crashed down another gear into first. The Mercedes was looming up fast but Moses had been slow enough into the bend for it to make a difference. In the back of the truck the wooden souvenirs were protesting and the trailer tyres were squealing, biting the tarmac to absorb the cargo's momentum. Moses hit the brake pedal a final time and held it down, so that when his front bumper touched Jacko's car it was travelling slowly enough, at less than a walking pace.

Moses didn't expect what happened next – the Mercedes began moving, imperceptibly at first, but then it had a rush as gravity took hold. The slow impact was enough to have nudged the barrier-end, admitting the Mercedes with its naked cargo into the natural abyss of the gorge. Muriel dashed towards her husband of twenty-seven years, but was still a way off as Jacko accelerated downwards through the thin and un-supporting air to oblivion.

Jacko's Boys

The Johannesburg Post

On Monday morning, four hundred feet above the heaving streets of Jozi, Bruce Pontin and I sat staring at the wall clock, just prior to ringing Hilton Clarke, the free-speaking mandarin with an intimate knowledge of ex-president de Klerk's political life.

"How was the wedding?"

"Good. They'll make a great couple." I said.

"Where are they honeymooning?"

"Not sure, off the Mozambique coast somewhere."

"Catch up with Rosy?"

"I did, but we didn't talk that much. Hopefully, we'll say hello again before she heads back to the UK."

"How was she?"

"Same as ever, but without me as her partner, well, incomplete, I'd say."

"That'll explain why she dumped you. The pursuit of incompleteness, makes total sense to me."

"Thank you for that, actually Rosy was strong. Very beautiful, same gamine haircut. Intellectually frightening, no, inspiring. Conspicuously trim, apparently she still jogs every day – then yoghurt, sunflower seeds, pumpkin seeds and flax, same old Rosy."

"Work?"

"Yeah, pretty senior at Silvermans' Bank in London. She spent a couple of years at the Chicago Commodity Exchange, learning how to buy and sell things, well, bullion, and then moved to London."

"And you stayed here to chase the truth and rewrite history."

"Yes, and you should be grateful."

Bruce smiled and rechecked the wall clock, nodding the go-ahead.

"Don't be overlong, let's hit the streets tonight."

"No worries, the piece is already written. I just need a few live quotes, and Andrew Mopeli hopes I can tempt

Hilton to confirm the existence of de Klerk's report."

"Hilton Clarke speaking, is that the Post?"

"Yes, good morning, Hilton. This is Tim Kitson, and I'm speaking with you on an open link with my editor, Bruce Pontin."

"Good morning to you both."

"Hilton, I very much enjoyed your book. It contains some entirely new insights. Tell me, when did President de Klerk first learn of the country's chemical and biological warfare programme?"

"It was part of his pre-inauguration briefing. De Klerk's policy objective at that time was to re-join the international community, that meant being signed up to the non-proliferation treaty. The biological weapons programme was incompatible with that and so he demanded it come to an end."

"You mentioned the international community. Is it true that London and Washington were so concerned they made an official protest?"

"Yes."

"What were their concerns?"

"They feared proliferation, and they feared that certain individuals would exacerbate things by selling what they knew to the highest bidder."

"What was de Klerk's view of chemical and biological warfare?"

"The same as his view on nuclear warfare. Tim, you should remember, de Klerk is still the only head of state ever to have ordered the destruction of his country's weapons of mass destruction – nuclear, biological, and chemical."

"That is a first, I agree. Hilton, why did de Klerk commission a report that was subsequently never made public?"

Apart from the amplified hum and an occasional crackle on the line there was silence. I looked at Bruce with raised eyebrows and a face of mock trepidation.

"I was never told, but I think the report was reclassified as secret due to the need for a confidential overview, triggered by the discovery of criminality among the military. After receiving the report de Klerk briefed the top brass and between them they took immediate action, removing individuals and in some cases firing whole lists of people."

I smiled at Bruce and he gave me the thumbs up.

"Can you tell us who those individuals were?" I said.

"No, I can't. Action was taken to ensure individual names were never released. There is a list of companies fronting the programme."

"What happened to the report and its classified information?"

"De Klerk was provided with a key to a safe, which could only be unlocked with two keys, and in which the information was stored."

"Who had the second key?"

"It was held by state security."

"Hilton, thanks very much, that's all very interesting."

"Hang on, Tim, a précis of the report was made available to Jacko, he insisted on having a copy. Afterall, it was essentially about Jacko's boys, the Recces."

Township Millionaires

Mossel Baai

While Theo Mason delivered the best-man's speech, Moses stood at the road side startled by the appearance of an out-of-nowhere police officer, who materialised at the scene of the collision within moments of it happening, scrabbling down an embankment with the agility of a mountaineer. Broad-shouldered and chunky, with short-cropped hair, blue eyes, and a large, silver incisor, he introduced himself as Gary Roper.

"You must not worry, I saw the whole incident from the air, there was nothing you could have done."

Roper began collecting Jacko's discarded personal effects, before asking Moses for his details and offering to escort home a distraught Muriel. Moses found the experience disquieting. He wasn't even sure there would be an attempt at recovery, the man and his car were down there, somewhere, in the river, in the rapids. Moses got on his knees to inspect the lorry's bumper, which he was pleased to see was undamaged. When he removed his sunglasses to check the underside he was surprised to see an attaché case, lodged against the inside edge of the cab's front axle.

A policemen out of nowhere, and then a sobbing woman, equally magicked into place. Before that a car with a naked driver, and now an attaché case. Moses felt a deep sense of confusion. He didn't want to touch the case, yet he had no choice – he slid it under the passenger seat, hiding it mainly from himself.

Eventually, Moses reached his destination, had Constance unloaded by the warehouse guys and then drove off via a drankwinkle to the Bhunya motel on the outskirts of town. Once checked in he pulled the tab on a cold beer, and sitting at the room's rickety table, with a sense of misgiving, a stout screwdriver from his toolbox, and somebody else's property, he forced the attaché case locks.

When the lid flipped open, he gasped.

With a face of stone, Moses stared at what turned out to be $4.25m. He felt a need to throw up – he was into something deeply sinister and, knowing he was incapable of returning the money, something deeply threatening. He grabbed a few bales at random and ran his thumb across the bill ends. For a while he was gawping and motionless, but then his stomach began shaking and he stood up away from the table and gulped some beer. He twitched with a small scream, as if perhaps he'd trodden barefoot on an unsuspecting mouse. It was beyond Moses to convert the dollars into the currency of lorriness, or happiness. He sensed that danger swirled all around him, and with an infinite gravity, and he wondered what another might do to repossess what he had accidentally acquired. The noise in his head was tumultuous. It took no time for Moses to realise he wasn't going home again, ever, having given his name and address to a policeman.

Shit! Home!

Moses rang Jabu who didn't pick up.

∞

Under the cash were two reports, one entitled Third Force and the other, Project Costa. Moses flicked through the pages of Third Force, astonished, then horrified, by the abuse, the sorrow, the death. This was really something, some big shot in the military saying the military did these awful things.

Moses reached for his phone as it rang.

"How you doing?" Jabu said. "You gotta problem?"

"Yeah, I got a problem."

"I thought you must have, didn't expect to hear from you."

"We both got a problem Jabu. Now listen up. You need to come and meet me. You need your passport, and you need to meet me on the Mozambique border at Komatipoort. Don't bother to pack, just start out, now."

"What you on, Moses? You can't take Constance 'cross the border."

"I'm leaving her at Komatipoort."

"Moses, you fucking with me again? You trying to get out of buying me a truck, or something? She'll be stripped naked overnight you leave her at the border."

"Jabu, get out of the house. It's dangerous."

"I ain't doing that 'less you tell me what's going on Moses. Shit, there's someone messing with the door handle."

"Don't open it, Jabu."

"What the fuck is happening, Moses?"

And then Jabu recognised the unmistakable thudding whistle of a bullet released through a silencer, and the metallic ricocheting of its progress through the door lock.

He sprang up and ran, yelling.

"Moses, these boy's is shooting. What has you done?"

Jabu's question exploded into the still air of the night as the expiring telephone cord snatched the handset from his grip. Jabu burst into the darkness and tore through the backyard, and he flew over the fence, agile as a gazelle, faster, much faster, than his pursuer.

∞

Moses paced the short length of the motel room with a puzzled mind and a heart that beat like a Djembe. He wondered at one point whether the money could be forged, so that having escaped to Mozambique there would be nothing. But no, that wasn't it. The Kimbos were now a rare breed; they were township millionaires, in need of a vanishing act, true, but they were the richest black bastards in the country. They also needed to stash the money somewhere – pushing it across the counter to a bank teller was a no, no.

After a short while, Moses had thought about and fondled the money enough. Sitting astride one corner of the bed, he re-examined the reports – the ironically named Civil Co-operation Bureau was involved in assassinating political opponents, and they contaminated enemy drinking water with yellow fever and cholera. Cigarettes and chocolates were laced with anthrax spores, and there were killer dogs, epitomised by the vicious monster that was a genetic mix of Doberman, Rottweiler, and Bloodhound. Weighing in at over eighty-five kilos it was known as the Boerbul, a virtually uncontrollable mutant species trained to kill blacks.

When Moses read about the Centre for Scientific and Industrial Research he was forced to pull the tab on a third beer. In a programme that even the report described as bizarre, the centre had worked on a race-changing drug that would turn whites into blacks, so that apartheid operatives could infiltrate the ranks of the enemy – Moses was incredulous, the scale of things was beyond what any normal person could imagine.

"Fucking mad," he said.

Thumbing forward at random Moses recognised the name of Steve Biko, his figurative uncle.

"Black Consciousness, when we scorched Soweto onto the political landscape the world had to listen, had to witness the power of uncle Steve's philosophy."

Moses was still talking to himself when Jabu rang again.

"Where are you?"

"I'm in the office, crapping my trousers, brother. What the fuck's going on? Who is these people?"

"Jabu, I told you to get out of Hillbrow."

"You the one keeps my passport in the office safe."

"Oh fuck – just run for it, grab your passport and hit the border. I'm not sure what's going on. I think the same people killed Uncle Steve are up your arse."

"You told me there was no proof Uncle Steve was killed." Jabu said.

"I'm holding it."

"What you holding?"

"They poisoned him with thallium while they were torturing him."

"I never heard of thallium."

"Rat poison. Thins the blood. It's mistaken for haemorrhaging of the brain, murder disguised as an accident during a rough interrogation. Jabu, it says here that thousands of our black brothers died in police cells."

"Thousands! That makes me feel safe on the street, even tonight."

"Well, you're not. They know who I am, otherwise, they wouldn't have come to the house. If they know that much, they'll also know we have an office, so move it. Jabu I got some good shit to tell you, but not on the phone. Things are gonna be fine, it's gonna be great, just get up to Komatipoort."

Constantia Nek

Cape Town

Larry Lauderdale of the Chequers Bank was no ordinary manager. He'd been available 24/7 for his military clients, well colleagues, for as long as they could remember. So yesterday, when he took a call at home from Theo Mason, it was not exceptional."

"Morning Larry. How is it?"

"Fine, thank you."

"Good. Larry, sorry to bother you on a Sunday, but I have a problem."

"What sort of problem?"

"I had a speech to make at Stefan Taylor's wedding yesterday and I gave Smit the job of tracking Jacko. He came back empty-handed. Did Jacko keep his appointment with you yesterday?"

"Yes, eleven thirty, prompt, emptied the box, as we anticipated."

"Okay, so he had the contents with him."

"Definitely, took them away in an attaché case, cuffed to his wrist."

"Okay, Larry."

"Theo, while you're on the line. What was the thinking about Jacko's meeting with Chios?"

"As you've probably heard, from today we're a team member down."

"So it wasn't a road accident."

"A couple of years back when Jacko told us to dismantle things – liquidate the companies, destroy the stockpiles. There was something he didn't tell us."

"Shit. What?"

"De Klerk, I suppose in an attempt to tidy apartheid's grubby basement before the new black owners moved in, commissioned a report to ascertain exactly what we'd been up to, and because we did such a fantastic job the last thing anyone wants is knowledge of it reaching the public domain, and it would be a disaster if it did."

"Why so?"

"After all the promises of anonymity the Boss-man’s name is at the top, just above mine. My problem is that Jacko had a copy with him, collected from your vaults yesterday."

"So they don't know who we are yet, but anytime soon we're fucked."

"Yep, I need to find the report before it's exposed."

"Theo, before you go, I’m gathering the unconsolidated funds for last month and posting them to the transfer account. Perhaps you could pass that up the line and have an offshore deposit arranged?"

"Sure thing."

∞

"Smit, you incompetent shit, where’s the attaché case?" Theo said.

"The chopper video shows it in the road, next to the Mercedes, with Jacko slumped across the car's bonnet."

"So where the fuck is it, Smit?"

"I don’t know. Once I realised there was going to be a collision I set the chopper down and clambered over the embankment, and in no time. But Theo, there was nothing, no Mercedes, no Jacko, no attaché case."

Theo had the chopper’s video sent to him and played it several times, knowing full well that Smit should have hovered above the scene and not peeled off to land at such a critical moment. Either circumstance had combined to take the attaché case over the edge with the Mercedes, which looked unlikely, given its position on the road, or it had been removed. The second option narrowed the field to Muriel Jackson or the lorry driver, a Moses Kimbo, whose name had been taken by Smit. A brief conversation with Muriel was all it took for Theo to be left staring solemnly at the remaining name on his pad.

It was all lip-curlingly irksome.

"Mr. Moses, the Promised Land in which you intend to spend our money, you will never reach. I shall see to it myself, you FUCKWIT."

The Boerbul

Hillbrow

The brothers' office was small. Its most impressive asset was an oak swivel chair in which Jabu had huddled himself, reluctant to climb into his cold wreck of a Micra for a five-hour drive to Komatipoort. Jabu was rolling cigarettes, and falling from his trembling fingers was a fine tobacco leaf dust.

Jabu had been in some sticky states before but it was a long time since guns had chased him round town. He pulled a Zippo from his pocket, pushed a cigarette between his lips and thought for a moment. He decided Moses was in a real fix or he had something worth more than Constance, but on the telephone he was up. He's struck gold.

When Jabu thumbed the Zippo's flint wheel its petrol ignited in tandem with a hugely percussive bang that shook the office's corrugated iron roof and unhinged the door from its frame. Jabu swivelled on his chair towards the falling door as a brawny white man stomped into the office and moved swiftly towards him, so that when their eyes met, the muzzle of the intruder's gun was touching the smouldering end of Jabu's cigarette.

"You take your work very seriously Moses, it's past midnight."

"Who are you?" Jabu said.

"Don't worry about who I am, Moses. Worry about what I'm going to do to your black arse. Where's the fucking attaché case?"

"Put that gun down, man. Why you calling me Moses? I'm Jabu."

"Don't tell me what to do you black bastard. Answer the fucking question."

The human equivalent of the canine Boerbul thrust its chunky forearm and the gun barrel forward at an incredible speed, crumpling Jabu's cigarette before collecting three half-teeth and a chunk of top lip on a path to the back of his throat.

"Jabu who, by the way?"

There was pain and blood and, in order for Jabu to answer, a spluttered eviction of teeth and flesh from his mouth.

"Balloi." He said.

Jabu had no intention of saying Kimbo.

"And what the fuck are you doing here in the middle of the night, Mr. Balloi?"

Jabu hurt – he could feel the cold air rushing through the microscopic tunnels of his broken teeth to the nerve ends, and he didn't know whether he could think fast enough for this brute of a thing.

The Boerbul pulled back its forearm as if cocking the trigger of a gun, ready for a second shot. Jabu raised his hand as a reflex, blurting out that he was the night watchman who'd been guarding the truck.

"Please. I'm innocent. You've only just missed Moses. I don't know what he's done but you can find him heading south out of town. It's a big blue Volvo, you can't miss it. Please, don't hurt me again."

"How long ago did he leave?"

"No time. Ten, fifteen minutes."

Jabu was hoping to God he didn't get searched; just a glance at the passport nestled in his pocket would mean shit. He didn't know what to do with the teeth and flesh in his hand. It felt uncomfortable but the pieces were too personal to discard on the concrete floor, especially the fragments of his saxophone-playing teeth.

The intruder accepted what he heard laconically with nothing more than a grunt, the thought that he could catch Moses spurring him on. Even so, he placed the gun muzzle alongside Jabu's right ear and smiled, before pulling the trigger.

The View

Easthope

On a dream of a subtropical morning, Stefan Taylor coaxed a Ventura Battalion helicopter to five thousand feet, adjusted the autopilot and set off over an ocean of prickly mopane bush. Stefan's passenger was Theo Mason, his commanding officer, and the destination was The View, at that time run by Oliver Lennox. Theo had been tasked with acquiring a site suitable for the final trials of Rainmaker's research project, and a guava orchard owned by the Lennox family was a possible location.

Ninety minutes into the journey Stefan descended to fifteen hundred feet, and began rotating the chopper in a slow clockwise spin, while letting it fall gently at three hundred feet per minute.

"It's got everything we need, and a perfect location, can't be more than thirty miles to Mozambique." Theo said.

Hovering at two hundred feet they were unaware of Oliver below them, huddled from the helicopter rotors beneath the canopy of a guava. Oliver stood pondering the orchard's bleak future. Decimated the previous evening by hailstones the size of tennis balls, the trees had been flailed and the guavas pulped. Thirteen years of love and anticipation were gone in minutes, shot to bits in a hail of ice.

Stefan moved the chopper off and sat it down on the designated aitch at a nearby aerodrome, and they walked the tarmac to the terminal building. Theo placed a call to Rainmaker's chief weatherman and asked Stefan about the Lennox family while waiting.

"Ordinary people. Farmers, been here for a hundred years, reasonably wealthy, members of the Democratic Party." Stefan said.

"Hello, I'd like to know when it last hailed in Easthope – big ones." Theo said.

"Last night? Great! Thank you."

"Stefan, a taxi, I'll come through in a moment, after

I've called the farm."

∞

"How was it?" Emma said.

"Obliterated, total write-off."

"That's terrible, Dad."

"Maybe we'll replant."

"Think on it; think on it with a beer, that'll help. Dad, d'you know a Theo Mason? He's on his way up here to talk with you."

"Never heard of him, bring him out to the patio when he arrives."

After pulling the tab on a cold beer, Oliver threw a match at the fuelled charcoal on his barbeque and sat to consider the orchard. A short while later Emma appeared with their visitors.

"Dad, Theo Mason, Managing Director of Rainmaker, and his colleague, Stefan Taylor, their Operations Manager."

Stefan, who had stopped on the far side of the patio, smiled politely at Oliver as his name was mentioned.

"Shall I fix you a drink Stefan?" Emma said.

It was clear to her that she and Stefan were superfluous, and when he nodded they retraced their steps to the house.

"How can I help, Theo?" Oliver said.

Theo apologised for the intrusion, explaining the matter was urgent because of his imminent departure abroad, and described Rainmaker's requirement very simply – a site to test its groundbreaking technology. Oliver was absorbed but not really up to speed, and so asked for clarification.

"You make rain?" He said.

"We do, yes. That's what we do. It's a technique that introduces silver iodine molecules into clouds, cumulus typically, those that have formed large potentially crop-wrecking hailstones. The iodine molecules act as new nuclei to the ice deposits, which migrate from the hailstone and coalesce as rain droplets."

"Amazing," Oliver said.

"If we had been here yesterday we could have

turned the hailstones that wrecked your orchard into rain."

"Sangoma! Do you dance as well?" Oliver said.

"Mr. Lennox, I am not a witch doctor, or Sangoma as you say. I am a scientist representing the Government, in an area of great national, and probably international, importance."

"Yes, what's your proposal Mr. Mason?"

Within ten minutes they agreed terms. Rainmaker would use Oliver's land, primarily the devastated guava orchard, and have access across it to the aerodrome's runway, from which the company would operate two Bombardier Lear jets, converted for cloud seeding. Additionally, Rainmaker would require permission to install a long-range radar facility and erect a small administrative building and chemical store. In return Rainmaker would offer a rental stream, which Oliver found impossible to turn down.

∞

In the house, Emma and Stefan were drinking homemade lemonade and having their own conversation,.

"What are they talking about?"

"We, well, Rainmaker, would like to rent some of your farmland, adjacent the airfield."

"To do what?"

"Hum, do you know about the changing patterns of our global weather system?"

"A bit, I work in television and I recently interviewed a guy about the Gaia Hypothesis. I know the climate is changing, and is creating some pretty unpredictable and dangerous weather."

"You got it, exactly. James Lovelock's idea, accepting that planet Earth, well, mother Earth, Gaia, is a self-regulating, living, dynamic environment, is the current thinking.

"The guy I interviewed said we're polluting the atmosphere, or heating the atmosphere through polluting it, and to the extent that we're undermining Gaia's ability to self-regulate.."

"Unpredictable weather, you said. Others say catastrophic, droughts, wildfires, raising ocean temperatures, and huge melt water volumes at the icecaps."

"Blimey. Stefan, more lemonade?"

"Thanks. At Rainmaker we use Peru as a barometer to help predict the changing weather. It's a weird country, though – its main export is coca leaf, bought by cocaine manufacturers around the world."

"Ah, I did a programme on that as well. Illegal coca exports earn the country more that the fishing industry, which is second only in the world to China."

"Well, it's the fishing industry that we use as a barometer. Peru's coastal plain runs more or less parallel to the various cordilleras, and the coastal waters are unusually stable, offering the best breeding environment in the world for anchovy. In good times the anchovies will bunch together in their millions in the thermocline, the buffer zone between the upper and lower waters of the ocean."

"OK, ah, slowly?"

"Sure, there are complex interactions in all this chaos. So, easterly winds normally push warm surface waters in the equatorial Pacific towards Australia and Indonesia and away from Peru. As a result, warm water piles up in the west Pacific and cool water is drawn up from the depths of the east Pacific along the Peruvian coastline. This is the neutral state, and anchovy heaven – they form enormous, swirling bait balls, attracting snappers and bream. The smaller fish attract bigger fish like yellow fin tuna, which in turn bring in the marlin, followed by the sharks – that food chain is the fishing industry."

"And in the bad times?"

"Without a thermocline capable of supporting anchovies, which needs to be cooler rather than warmer, the food chain collapses, completely, and that's our barometer – a fall in fish stock signalling death in the anchovy population signals a change in the weather."

"What sort of change, and how does that work"

"So, right now, the ocean is hotter than normal, it's five degrees above normal. That triggers a change – in the eighteen nineties, when similar conditions were first recorded, and because it was Christmas, the phenomenon was associated with Jesus, the little boy – El Nino translates as the Christ Child. The increased ocean heat rises and interferes with the jet stream, and that has the effect of cancelling the westerly winds. An El Nino allows the warmed Pacific Ocean to slosh back towards Peru in one vast wave – it sinks the thermocline and kills the anchovies.

The present El Nino has knocked the entire jet stream off course. In Indonesia drought has taken down the world's largest coffee crop. In the Philippines farmers are erecting images of an infant Jesus in the fields, praying for rain. In Borneo the forest was set ablaze and is still burning, already seven-and-a half million acres are ash. In the Soviet Union, where drought has cracked the earth, the wheat harvest is failing and leaving millions on the verge of starvation."

"Yet the reverse happened in the States. The American corn barons have produced such a bumper harvest the price of wheat has fallen through the floor." Emma said.

"Don't tell me, you made a programme about it?"

"My sister Rosy works with the Chicago Commodity Exchange."

"Oh! Anyway, Rainmaker has patented a technique to both precipitate and stop rainfall. It began as a programme to eradicate the tennis ball sized hailstones brought to this region by the Antarctic airflows, like the ones that wrecked your dad's guavas. But the technique's capability has been extended to help drought conditions around the world, and we know it works, the technology is astonishing. We can make it rain more or less to order, but right now we need an operational base to carry out the final field tests."

"That is amazing. You know, Stefan, you don't seem like a businessman at all."

"You're very intuitive. I'm a soldier, seconded to Rainmaker. It's a business run by the military."

"And before?"

"I was a reconnaissance commando, a Recce. I still am a commando. Previously I operated across the Angolan border. Grim stuff. In the beginning I thought it was necessary. These days I think it stinks."

"Stinks?"

"Racism. War crimes. We would never treat our

own people the way we treated the Angolans. Apart from being black, we say they're communists or terrorists. Mostly, we pretend they're all three, black-communist-terrorists."

"War crimes?"

"Yeah, a place called Kassinga. It was hell. Emma, I'm still in the army. I can't say too much."

There in a Jiffy

The Johannesburg Post

I sat at my new desk with a bring-in coffee and an almond croissant, staring at a reasonable pile of assorted mail. There were also a few internal memos, and I had voicemails. By chance alone I had landed the best office in the building, atop the tall glass obelisk's northwest tower, overlooking a panoramic Jozi and, I bet you won't believe this, the largest manmade urban forest in the world – three million trees, planted by hand.

The mail rose to a vaguely pyramidal apex, determined by envelope size, and there was a large oversized Jiffy bag at the base.

My third voicemail was fantastic.

"Hi Tim, it was great to see you again after so long. You said we might get together but there's really only Wednesday. I'm defo up for it if you are. My flight is at eight that evening from Jan Smuts. Let me know what you think."

I intercomed Bruce.

"I know it's short notice but can I slip a day's holiday in tomorrow?"

"Short notice! You've only been here a matter of hours."

"I'm sure I could make it up."

"Let me think. Today's Tuesday, which means tomorrow is Wednesday, Rosy's last day in the country. Tim, is Thursday any good?"

"It's okay then?"

"If anybody asks, I'll tell them you're on an assignment. Enjoy yourself."

I took a sip of coffee and started on the mail, happy as a bunny. I had a secretary but for the first couple of weeks I wanted to sort it myself. There was a stack of readers' views, good, bad, and indifferent. A couple of social invitations, in my capacity as the Post's new political editor, a letter from the ANC asking for an introductory meeting, and loads of industry bumf, and a large brown

Jiffy bag, which I picked up and opened after dialling Rosy.

"Hi, I could fly you down to Jan Smuts," I said, "and perhaps we could stop off at the dam for lunch?"

"A picnic at the dam?" Rosy said.

"Yeah, that's what I had in mind."

"Fabulous, we haven't done that in years."

"Good. Hey, we didn't find much time to talk at the wedding. I didn't even ask about London. Do you prefer it to Chicago?"

"I probably do, and the work's okay, but somehow I think a change would be good, something out of banking."

"I've read about you in the financial press, you're the received wisdom on bullion since your time at the Chicago Corn Exchange and your work with Al Calascione."

I stuck my hand inside the Jiffy bag and grabbed its contents, but I was gazing aimlessly across the city, enthralled with the prospect of seeing Rosy, completely unaware of what I was holding.

"Tim, I was there, but Al Calascione was the hero, working mostly with my CEO, Toby Weinberg. What about you, journalism seems to have worked out?"

"It has."

Then I saw what I was holding, and the red Top Secret stamp.

"I'm never sure what'll happen next. Listen, I'll tell you all about it tomorrow, I need to go now."

It took no time to understand why the documents were stamped Top Secret, and each time I flicked from one report to the other – 'Third Force' and 'Project Costa' – the world made more sense. I worked out pretty quickly that although the two reports were linked, they represented entirely separate intrigues.

"Can I talk to you, Bruce?"

"Sure, take a seat. Oh, don't tell me she turned you down."

"That's not what I want to talk about, and she said yes."

"What have you got there?"

"I've got the scoop of the year. I've got Jacko's report, the précis."

"The report Hilton Clarke talked about?"

"Yeah. Plus, there's a second report by General

Fulsoma, no less, analysing the deployment and sale of chemical and biological warfare agents. Fulsoma's report is a full-blown exposé on an operation code-named Project Costa."

"Where did you get them?"

"The postman."

"Really?"

"Bruce, I don't understand the secrecy. Our black politicians could use a whole lot of this stuff to their advantage. Like, apparently, there's an eyewitness account of Steve Biko's murder."

"You're kidding me!"

"No, I'm not, and hang on, another witness explains how we assassinated Samora Machel."

"Wow! How credible are the witnesses?"

"I haven't assessed that yet, and there are very few names. Anyway, what intrigues me is why has this been sat on, and whatever the reason, it's news, news, news. Bruce, the Fulsoma report, it's fucking unbelievable. We produced chemical and biological warfare agents not only in contravention of the Non-Proliferation Treaty but we sold them internationally. We sold warheads to Libya. Libya of all fucking places! And it looks likely Libya sold some of them on to Iraq. Remember Halabja? Well I hope it wasn't South African nerve gas that wiped out 5000 Kurds."

Bruce's phone rang.

"Tim, Jane says there's a Jordan Atwell on the line for you."

"Sout Peel? Ask her to take a number. I'll get back to him."

"Jane, take a number, Tim's busy. Thanks."

"Sout Peel?" Bruce said.

"That's his nickname in the lowveld. Salty Dick. You should improve your Afrikaans. A fence-sitter, a person with one foot in the Republic of South Africa and one foot in the UK, with his dick in the Atlantic, Salty Dick. He's the big honcho in Pan African Commerce, built a solid reputation on his ability to facilitate interstate trade. Mind you, a few years back I reckon he was sanctions busting."

"Back to the reports. What else?" Bruce said.

"Right, there are two reports. The Third Force report is an itemised account of bloody massacres – Jacko's boys at their gory worst. And then the other report, about Project Costa, which as Clarke said, was secretly funded through an array of front companies – Alpha Laboratories, Rainmaker, Omega E – is about the development and manufacture of chemical and biological warfare agents."

"Do you still think you're having tomorrow off?"

"Yes, it needs thinking through. I'll make a copy and take it with me."

"Tim, it all happened before the black Government came to power."

"Yes, I reckon de Klerk started dismantling the programme but it ran on, maybe two, three years."

"Into the new Government?"

"Yeah, and that's their embarrassment. I'll tell you something else, there's been no verification of what happened to the stockpiles."

∞

"Jordan, it's Tim Kitson. You rang."

"Yes, your piece last night, interesting, particularly Clarke's allegation that the Government used a string of front companies. As I think you know, I'm President of Pan African Commerce. I'm concerned some of our members may be implicated. Can you help me?"

"The companies have all since been wound up."

"Mr. Kitson, I don't want to be indelicate but are you able to give me any names?"

"There is a list of companies, but I don't think it's appropriate to reveal names at this stage."

"Clarke gave you the names in confidence?"

"Clarke gave us the background, the specific company names came from General Fulsoma. He compiled a report to which the Post has gained access."

"Quite a scoop. In tonight's paper?"

"We don't publish without corroboration. I'll probably put the listing together for Thursday."

"I look forward to it, and if you need any assistance in profiling these companies, I'd be only too pleased to help."

∞

I made a second call and got hold of Andrew Mopeli.

"You were right, what you said at the wedding." I

said.

"About walking through shit?"

"That as well. But no, you were right about the existence of a secret report."

"When I borrowed Joshua Chios from the justice department he came with a categorical assurance that no such report existed. Tim, you've heard about Jackson?"

"Yes, no longer your star witness, but he may still be able to help. I have his copy of the de Klerk report.

"What?"

"Arrived in the post, anonymously."

"Fantastic. Are you willing to let me see it?"

"Of course, but it'll cost you dinner, and an introduction."

"You don't mean Chios?"

"Yes, I feel obliged to hear why he mislead the eminent Andrew Mopeli?"

"OK, if you can make down to the Cape, come tomorrow to the Members' dining room in the Parliament Buildings, around eight. I've already arranged to meet Chios at eight thirty, we can talk things through before he arrives."

"Sure thing. I'm flying Rosy to Jan Smuts tomorrow so I'll catch a scheduled flight after seeing her off to the UK.

Romeo

Easthope

That evening after work, and after completing my pre-flight checks and obtaining take off clearance from air traffic control, I eased our syndicate-shared Cessna off the Jozi runway in a shallow climb over the Highveld and Witwatersrand. The sierra-toothed ridge of mountains below me contained the richest gold deposits in the world, buried deep in underground seams between other geologies of coal and manganese.

At Witbank the highveld merges with the middleveld, which continues for a few miles before plunging over the escarpment into the lowveld. From there it's a short hop through the valley to Easthope, hometown for both my folks and the Lennox family. In less than an hour I was putting on a few degrees of flap and straightening for my final approach, listening to crackle of Marty Schwartz's voice, welcoming me home and clearing me for landing. Officially, Marty had nothing to do with the control tower, but the small aerodrome was relaxed and easy-going, and for him to be on the approach frequency talking his friends down was nothing unusual. Marty's real expertise was in aero engineering and in flying helicopters where nobody else could. He owned Schwartz Aero Services, a local paint and repair outfit which he ran with his wife Dixie from two hangers on the aerodrome's perimeter.

After landing I parked the Cessna at the far end of hangar five and chocked the wheels, before walking over to Marty's office. It was obvious he was doing well – infillings on the wall planners showed a busy workload, and a bank of new computers and office furniture said it was profitable.

"Hi Marty, how is it?"

"Pretty good. Gees, you're looking strong yourself. Are you going to drink your beer, Tim?"

"What beer?"

"In the fridge there, been waiting for you to come

home and pull the tab."

"How many beer fridges you got these days? Hey, when do I need to have Oscar back?"

Schwartz checked the syndicates schedule and I stooped to grab a beer.

"Martin de Veer has him on Friday for a fishing trip. We'll need a routine service beforehand, which means being back for midday Thursday. If that's manageable, Oscar's yours. What's on?"

"Said I'd collect Rosy from Skukuza and fly her down to Jozi."

"Tim, you could have taken my crop sprayer if you needed a set of wings."

"Thank you, but Oscar's not quite as eye-watering as your open top croppy."

"Zulu Oscar Romeo Delta," Schwartz began. "Zulu designates South Africa, and the rest is Oscar's call sign."

"I know, why are you telling me that?"

"I think we should give the other letters a chance. So, shall I get one of the boys to fuel up Romeo for you?"

"Oh, piss-off. Anyway, that would be great, thanks."

∞

"Hi Dad, just to let you know I'm in Easthope but I won't make it over tonight."

"No problem, catch you next time. That was a great piece in the Post about Hilton Clarke's new book and the de Klerk report. That stuff has been waiting on the side-lines for years. The rumours were circulating in Pretoria before I quit the justice system, so well done, getting it into the public domain."

My dad spent his life wresting innocent blacks from the apartheid court system. The combination of his innate blarney and an unerring grasp of jurisprudence made him famous among the liberal whites and the black community for his successes and infamous among the Afrikaners for exactly the same reasons.

"The next trick is finding out what happened to the money." He said.

"What money?"

"Ah, son, I thought you were the investigative

journalist."

"Dad, what money?"

"The rumour said hundreds of millions were misappropriated by the Reconnaissance Commandos, they were secretly selling warfare agents and trousering wads of dosh at the same time."

"What else do you know?"

"Will I get a by-line? Just joking. Ah, well, not much, the criminality within the military was extensive, that's probably it. Would you like to speak to your mother?"

"Thanks Dad."

Mum wondered, quite simply, whether I had seen that nice Lennox girl, aware as she spoke of parodying the type of mother she could never be. I said not much but might, and left it at that, and after a five-minute chat rang off and settled for the evening with a note pad. I taught myself, in those rookie at The Herald, years, to read between the lines, omissions often became statements of intent, but in the two reports there were no step-this-way signs, and, intriguingly, no talk of money. There was a section on secret funding but not misappropriated funds, and so I dog-eared the start page of a section on illicit drugs and stopped reading.

∞

Next morning I confirmed with Rosy the weather was fine for flying, and that we could stop off at the dam, have a picnic, before flying on down to Jozi to connect with her flight home to the UK. We arranged to meet outside the Game Park's terminal building – a shack, in reality.

"Rosy, I'll meet you at ten but don't be late. It's so busy with tourists these days I had to book a take-off slot. It's for ten forty-five, if we miss it we'll be there for hours. How are you?"

"I'm fine, looking forward to seeing you. I'm a bit done in this morning though, should have got to sleep earlier."

"And what were you up to that kept you from sleeping?"

"Actually, I was getting sweaty with Peter Lipscombe."

"Lipscombe! I thought that was over years ago."

"Well, I suppose it was over, but last night we were

at it for a couple of hours. The climax was unbelievable, we were both lost in its purring depths."

"I can't believe you're telling me this."

"I suppose it must sound strange, but don't worry, I can explain."

"Fine, see you at ten."

∞

Oscar was parked on the grass, refuelled and ready to go. As all pilots do, I strolled round the aircraft prior to take off checking for physical damage or anything untoward. When it came to kicking the tyres to confirm their pressure I gave the first one a particularly hard boot.

Romeo, that is a fucking joke. Peter fucking Lipscombe. Bloody weed, poncy banker.

The second tyre got a Herculean kick that rocked the whole aeroplane.

"Steady, something wrong?" Marty said.

"Rosy's been sleeping with that poncy Lipscombe, getting sweaty all night. Why would she tell me that?"

Marty smiled and began laughing.

"What's so bloody unfunny?" I said.

"You've forgotten how she winds you up, and it works every time 'cos you're so besotted. If Rosy's been shagging Lipscombe I'll eat my hat and the little hair that's beneath it, and I'll give you the largest beer fridge. Just get over to Skukuza and pick her up."

"Well I hope you're right. If you're not, there's an expensive bottle of champagne going to waste."

"Don't go drinking champagne while you're flying Oscar, sorry, Romeo."

"Get back to work Marty, I'll see you later. And you had better launder that hat and wash your hair."

A few years later when the world changed and international passenger jets began landing at Easthope, security became an issue and the casual nature of the place changed forever. A large perimeter fence appeared and Marty couldn't get anywhere near the control tower without a photo ID and an entry code for the electronic doors.

Yet last night, the aerodrome was the open, accessible place it always had been, and a professional murderer walked through the complex and towards hangar five feeling entirely comfortable in the knowledge he wouldn't be challenged. The practised killer spent a leisurely few minutes arming a wedge of Semtex, before embedding his handiwork in the underside of the pilot's seat, my seat – not that I knew anything about it when I was kicking the tyres. A source in Jozi had leaked my flight plan, Easthope – Skukuza – Jan Smuts, and provided the timings.

An hour's flying from Skukuza would have Rosy and I on an approach to the escarpment, and at precisely eleven forty-five, Oscar would suddenly lose height and disintegrate on the steep face of the plateau – clearly, pilot error. Luckily, the baddies knew nothing about our picnicking history and the planned stopover.

Bang

Oliver's Dam

Rosy drove to Skukuza along the Sabie River, through maple-leafed mopane bush and herds of bushbuck and buffalo, arriving just before ten. We met in the airfield waiting lounge and hugged each other hello, although on my part I did it suspiciously, and we walked off towards the private pilot's gate, where a small transit vehicle was waiting to carry us out across the tarmac.

"It's great to see you. Do you still want to picnic at the dam. Perhaps you'd prefer to fly straight to Jan Smuts?" I said.

"Yes, of course, I'm looking forward to the picnic. Why do you think I wouldn't want to stop over?"

"Some of what you said this morning."

"Oh, I'll explain that when we get there."

"I'm not sure I want to know."

"It's ten thirty."

"OK, I'm on it." I said.

When I leant across to fully engage Rosy's door lock I felt a playful hand move through my hair. I was stretched and face down over Rosy's lap – there were flashes of mental chaos, and a rekindled desire set ablaze in an instant. I came upright mentally wowing, and slowly touched my way tentatively through the pre-take-off routine. After gaining the tower's permission for start-up and manoeuvring I began taxiing towards the runway.

Forty minutes later we were heading southwest towards the escarpment face in a shallow climb, sufficient to clear the ridge and reach the plateau. A few minutes later we popped over the crest and saw the small grass strip directly ahead, running alongside Oliver's dammed water. The lake's lacustrine peace, with its gently rippling surface, a profusion of water lilies and the odd aquatic plant, was beautiful.

Oscar's tyres scuffed the grass at a hundred knots and I pumped the brakes. According to the aircraft's clock I climbed down from the cabin fifty-seven minutes out of

Skukuza.

"Come out this side, I'll race you. Last one with their feet in the water gets to serve lunch."

Rosy retrieved her backpack and clambered over the seats. Yet as she moved across the leather her sandal snagged in the narrow aisle.

"Tim, I need some help. My foot's stuck, come and unhook me."

"Hang on, how can you be stuck?" I said.

Yet after walking round Oscar's prop to Rosy's side I could see what had happened.

"You're stuck on the upholstery anchor rod. Whoever cleaned the seat cover last put it back incorrectly. The easiest thing is for me to unbuckle your sandal."

Which I did, and then I held on tight to Rosy's bare foot and tickled its arch. In an instant she was writhing in the seat.

"Stop it!"

I learnt later that the Semtex timer was hidden a few centimetres from my face. Had it been clockwork I might have heard the ticking but it was digital, and accurate, running twenty seconds ahead of Oscar's own clock.

There were forty-five silent ticktocks remaining.

"I could be persuaded, but then again I could carry on tickling for a minute or two," I said.

"Stop it. I'll race you to the lake."

"I'll think about it."

Rosy composed herself and looked down at me.

"Peter Lipscombe doesn't and wouldn't tickle my feet." she said.

"Poncy banker. OK, let's go."

Rosy took off her second sandal and packed both in her backpack, fumbling with the straps and taking forever, before climbing down and throwing the rucksack on her back.

"Ready, steady, go." She said.

I went on a false start, a good half-second before

the go, and Rosy called me back.

"Cheat," she said.

"I won't do it again."

"Ready, steady, go."

And we were off, running towards the top of the lake’s gentle embankment, a hundred metres from Oscar’s wing tip. I was amazed to see Rosy streak off ahead, pulling away from me for the whole distance until she disappeared over the embankment's lip and began digging her heels in to avoid swimming with the fish and the lilies.

Travelling faster than Rosy, in fact faster than the speed of sound, the supersonic blast wave from the Semtex took a fraction of a second to cover the same distance. The explosive fireball scorched the earth as it zoomed towards the lake, and me. I reached the embankment as the pressure wave hit solidly between my shoulders and threw me forward into the grip of gravity. I flew over the embankment at an enormous speed, dropping the picnic hamper while being pursued by a large delta-shaped piece of flaming metal. There was such a rapid rise in temperature that the fireball never caught me, it gave up the horizontal chase and accelerated vertically through the cooler air for several hundred feet – a huge, billowing mass of pulsing orange-and-red energy.

I felt the explosion rolling over me, a mass of asphyxiating oxygen-depleted air, incomprehensibly hot, and then wet. Water was dragged from the lake’s surface and sucked upwards in a super-heated convection, then seconds later warm sheets of it crashed down all around me, and some of Oscar’s smouldering remains hit the lake.

I clambered down the embankment shaking wildly, fighting for breath.

"Christ! Are you all right?" I said.

"I think so, Jesus! How about you?"

"I’m okay. Thing is, Rosy, aircraft don’t do that, explode!"

"So, what the hell happened?"

"Someone just tried to kill us. If we had flown on we'd be spread across the escarpment face right now."

A convulsive shiver move across Rosy's body – I thought she may have visualised the escarpment’s granite, head-on at two hundred miles an hour.

"Who would do that?"

"I don't know. Jesus, if we hadn't landed – splat." I said.

"A convincing accident?"

"Yeah, Rosy, that's it – let's help the bastards think they succeeded."

I stood up and took off my shirt.

"Rosy, take your top off, rip it, throw some clothes in the lake. It might help them believe we're dead. And put your sandals on, we need to move. Checkout the hamper too, I hope the champagne's in one piece, back in a mo."

I crawled up the embankment and peaked over the top. Apart from a heat-distorted undercarriage leg and a smoking engine, Oscar had all but disappeared. Small fires were scattered all around, burning in the shade of a towering black pall of combusted kerosene.

I slid back down the embankment to find Rosy tossing her knickers into the lake.

"They look expensive." I said.

"They were, but the alternative, impersonating a bunny girl, going topless, it didn't appeal."

We were looking at each other, smiling – then I heard it.

"Shit, that was quick. Rosy, follow me. Let's go. It's a chopper."

I started off around the lake's perimeter, towards a dense spinney of conifers on the far side of the water. We passed a thin line of mango, and a coppice of hazel that Oliver had seeded to supply endless firewood for the braai. After a short distance, the helicopter's thundering rotors rose over the ridge and the pilot hovered into position above the mangos.

At the sight of rotor blades, Rosy gasped, and then accelerated, shouting as she passed for me to run faster.

"Tim keep up! What the fuck's going on here?"

The chopper's passenger was surveying Oscar's smouldering remains, and the bits of clothing and other debris bobbing in the lake, and I guess he was happy with his handiwork. Luckily for us, the pilot's angle of hover meant the assumed-dead were unseen running beneath it, before we sprang headlong into the woodland and moved fast through its semidarkness for a good distance, until we reached the half-light of a small clearing.

We fell to our knees, panting and exhausted. It seemed entirely natural to hold each other. Rosy said she could feel the pounding of my heart, and I could feel her hands on the skin of my wet, shirtless back. I was aware of her breasts too, touching me through the damp cotton of her blouse. Such closeness was hypoxic, displacing the little oxygen still in my blood. We keeled over into the dank vegetation, panting heavily from the sprint, and neither of us stirred. Finally we made eye contact – it was impossible not to kiss, and Rosy gathered me into a familiar and well-remembered togetherness.

I learnt later that laying there in the vegetation, Rosy was shackled to an agony of doubt – realising she still loved me, yet aware that she may be pregnant.

I certainly couldn't have guessed her concerns from the way she joked.

"A perfect day so far," she said. "Can't wait for this afternoon action. Tell me, do we think our assailants have spiked the picnic champagne with the deadly brown excrement of a Chinese grasshopper, or shall we drink it?"

"Let's drink it, pooh or not." I said.

"Tim, why I'm sitting in the semidarkness, without any knickers, without any luggage or possessions and, presumably, still with every chance of being bumped-off."

"I don't know. It might be that some individuals implicated in the reports I'm working on think they've been named."

"What reports?"

"Very sensitive reports, detailing a mass of high level skulduggery."

"What do you mean, think they've been named. Haven't they?"

"There are a few insignificant names, but none of the real baddies are identified. I might come up with some names investigating the front companies that were involved, perhaps that's making them jumpy, the idea I could eventually identify them."

"Front companies?"

"Yes, I can only guess what they did. Richardson Pharmaceuticals, well, drugs, presumably? The Rainmaker

Corporation, who knows, apart from the obvious, which is a daft idea."

"No, they did, they made rain," Rosy said.

I was startled, then annoyed as she repeated Dad's line.

"Tim, I thought you were the investigative journalist."

"That ain't funny. How do you know about Rainmaker?"

"They carried out field tests at the farm. It didn't last long, a couple of years I think. That's how Stefan and Emma got to know one another."

"Jesus, they made rain?"

"Yes."

I handed Rosy a glass and raised my own.

"Cheers, Rosy, good health."

"Very funny."

"Now, shall I call us a taxi?"

"What?"

"I assume you still want to get to Jozi."

I grabbed the aircom radio from my flight bag and punched in Jan Smuts' transit frequency.

"This is ground station Zulu Oscar Romeo Delta. Request relay message."

To Rosy's amazement there was an immediate reply. "Oscar Romeo Delta, this is Zulu Sierra Uniform Bravo, en route from Jozi to Phalaborwa, receiving you readability four. Pass your message."

"Good afternoon, Sierra Uniform Bravo. Message for Easthope Tower, on frequency one, one, niner decimal two. Oscar Romeo Delta down at Oliver's dam. Request Schwartz Aero Services' immediate helicopter support and onward transit to Jozi. Ground station Oscar Romeo Delta, contact frequency, one, zero, niner decimal five."

The pilot twelve thousand feet above us, flying a modern Dash 8 Turbo prop, read back the frequencies for confirmation, and then signed off saying he was glad to have helped.

"I must try that in London when I need a taxi." Rosy said.

"It wouldn't work, you're not trained in radio

telegraphy."

Marty was on the radio in no time, asking if we were both safe and whether the problem was fixable in situ. When Rosy overheard the question she slapped a hand over her mouth to avoid an audible fit of the giggles. I found myself saying it was doubtful and why didn't we talk about it when he arrived.

We didn't have to talk about it – Marty hovered over the lake and he could see Oscar's remains, much of it still smouldering.

"I'm not even going to ask about the underwear in the lake. How the shit did you get out of that?" Marty said.

∞

In Jozi, Marty sat the chopper down close up to the terminal building, helped us out and said goodbye.

"I won't come in, I feel obliged to get back and have a compassionate word with Martin de Veer, to explain that Oscar won't be going fishing this weekend. By the way, I know you owe me an aeroplane but do I owe you a beer fridge?"

"Good question, I'll keep you posted." I said.

My flight to Cape Town for the meeting Andrew Mopeli was at four fifteen, time enough for a coffee and a farewell chat with Rosy.

"Tim, it's been wonderful seeing you again, and it's been a great day, although challenging, runs against the instinct to live life to the full."

"Rosy, you're intelligent, you could warm to the idea of an early death, in exchange for quality time with me, surely."

"Part of that's true, I'm obviously intelligent."

Rosy lent across the table and placed her hand on my shoulder.

"I'm surprised at how fond of you I still am, it wasn't obvious to me, but seeing you again, I realise."

"Yeah." I said.

With a gentle nod, I stood to leave, looking uncharacteristically shrimpy in Marty's borrowed, oversized shirt. I blew Rosy a kiss, happy in the knowledge that Schwartz could keep his hat, his hair and his beer fridge.

A Slimy Leviathan

Cape Town

My airbus turned a broad arc over Table Bay and lowered its undercarriage. I stared at the water below, thinking of Rosy boarding her flight home to London. Beneath me, just off Cape Town's western shoreline, Robben Island slid in to view – where, nowadays, the residual spirits of a thousand black brothers welcomed tourists for refreshments in the prison yard and a tour of the cells.

I had booked a hotel room close to the parliamentary restaurant where I was to meet Andrew Mopeli. I strolled a short distance through the botanical gardens and sprang up the building's steps towards its entrance two at a time, where I surprised myself by almost colliding with Dorothy Tutani.

"Tim."

"Dorothy."

"Hi Tim, what are you doing here?"

"I've popped down to have a chat with Andrew."

"Jozi to Cape Town, that's a thousand-mile pop. Important chat?"

"Maybe. He's going to have Joshua Chios with him. Do you know him?"

"Yes, I know him. He's a one-off post-apartheid slimy Leviathan. If black elites replace white elites in this country, he'll be one of the first to take a seat at the table. You know, he's personable enough but totally transparent, he lives in a Chios-centric universe."

"That nice? Blimey. Hey, have you heard of The Rainmaker Corporation? Apparently they operated in Easthope."

Dorothy looked at me weirdly. There was a long silence and I realized it was an awkward question. I could see her deciding which way to play it.

"Is that what you're going to discuss with Chios?"

"Not really, Rainmaker's more of a side issue."

"Not for me, Tim. I'm in the process of suing them for tens of millions – compensation for constituency farmers."

"Rainmaker still exists?"

"Not any longer but I'm suing the Government who owned Rainmaker, and Chios is leading their legal team. He has a string of reasons to keep the whole thing under wraps, and he's refusing to acknowledge any liability."

"What did Rainmaker do wrong?"

"It's not a short story. Basically they trialled a virulent defoliant, spraying the fields in and around Easthope. Chios' defence is that Rainmaker was seeding clouds with sodium iodine in an experimental programme to precipitate rain and dissipate the outsized artic hail. Yet my constituents' evidence is pretty compelling. The farmers corelated field-test dates with prevailing distribution factors, like wind speed and direction, and matched their crop damage to the test dates every time – when rain hit the fields the crops fell over."

"Jesus, that's frightening. Dorothy, can I catch you tomorrow, I'm here until midday?"

"Sure, long as you haven't developed a proclivity for slimy Leviathans. I can fill you in on the details. Off the record, obviously.

∞

I presented myself at reception, stuck the ID badge given me to my lapel and made my way to the dining room. I was taken aback by the corridor walls, even after a few years of black rule they were covered with images of once-powerful white politicians. A gesture of magnanimous tolerance from Mandela's grouping, in stark contrast to the ransacking and overnight street renaming that followed the end of white supremacy in other African states. I stopped briefly to look at a portrait of Jacko, beaming down from an oiled canvas, the extent of his glittering oral bullion as remarkable as ever.

"I've got your reports, you old bastard."

I said it aloud, ridiculously, before walking on to the dining room, where the maître d'hôtel read my badge and welcomed me.

"Good evening Mr. Kitson. Mr. Chios is still to arrive but Mr. Mopeli is waiting for you. Follow me, sir."

I took a seat, ordered an aperitif, and listen to

Andrew.

"I was convinced the report existed. Well done. I can't understand it being kept from the Ethics Committee – the information should be entirely in the public domain."

"I agree, some of it makes gruesome reading but the new political order is in the clear. Andrew, one reason for stalling could be that something is still going on."

"I look forward to Chios' take on that. We've thirty minutes before he shows. What else is in those reports?"

I talked of state-sponsored murder, and mentioned some of the victims by name. A parcel bomb – Ruth First, a white anti-apartheid activist opening the morning post. A car bomb – Joseph Ntuli, a member of the Poqo underground movement, travelling to evensong with his wife. The poisons – the Reverend Frank Chikane escaped but many didn't. The lethal injections – Daniel Bakulu, a leading resistance figure, pierced with a spiked walking stick attending a rally in Natal. The infectious diseases, cholera and anthrax used to contaminate water supplies, taking out whole groups of people in a single hit, and the individual bullets in the back of the head.

"Andrew, I don't want to tell you this but I have no choice. There's a witness statement detailing the assassination of Samora Machel."

He stared at me.

"Then it details the murder of my wife."

"Yes."

Andrew maintained eye contact – silent, lost for the words which would meaningfully express his fury and sadness at what Jacko and his boys had done.

∞

As you know, before writing this book I re-interviewed many people, and that included Andrew. He and I talked at length about his wife's death in the air crash that killed the President of Mozambique. During that interview he was incapable of escaping a whirlpool of memories, and for a short while ceased to hear me at all. Andrew said he heard instead the words of his wife during their last conversation.

"It's going fine," Portia had said. *"I'm straight in at the deep end with the new job, and from Malawi I'm*

coming home via Mozambique."

"Portia, I talked to Abdul in Nairobi last week. He told me that a South African delegation had visited Malawi to express solidarity and discuss how to overthrow President Machel of Mozambique. So, take it easy."

"Don't worry; I'll be back for Thursday, latest. If I can hitch a ride to Mozambique later today, instead of flying scheduled tomorrow, I'll be home earlier, depends on a contact squeezing me onboard. How's the book?"

"It's done, Ubuntu is about to take the world by surprise."

"Everybody I meet, I tell them about it."

"Good – those who reckon there's no such thing as society need to know that people realise their humanness through other people, and that, in Ubuntu, is society.

"Andrew, we believe that, but it doesn't translate into Afrikaans."

"Sooner or later it will have to, or the whites will be hung out like biltong to cure under the sun."

"Maybe – I suspect Mandela, and you'll probably help him because of what you are, will forgive them all. I should go, a lot to do."

"Okay. Portia, congratulations. I hope the new job's as good as you thought it could be – what you've achieved is just great."

Andrew said that after a few seconds of schmaltzy kiss-blowing, their conversation ended, but forever.

A short while after that conversation, Portia took a call from her contact, Samora Machel's liaison secretary, who offered her a seat with the presidential entourage.

∞

In the report I was holding at the table that evening, as we waited for Joshua Chios to join us, the witness statement detailing the assassination of Samora Machel was clear, and gruesome. It said that Jose Bronco, having done what he had been paid to do, lay quiet and lifeless beneath Maputo airport's cluster of radio masts. One of Jacko's boys had encircled him with silent death, and the steel garrotte had forced a stiffened tongue from the victim's mouth as he expired. Jose had spent the last hours of his life reprogramming the airport's VOR transmitter, setting it to turn off for a critical period so that the signal from Maputo's homing beacon stopped. An alternative beacon installed on a hillside at Mbuzini in the Lebombo Mountains would then begin its transmission, pretending to be home.

Inbound to Maputo, the co-pilot of Samora Machel's Russian-built Tupolev, registered the decoy beacon in the mountains and initiated a premature turn, thinking nothing of it because he was already talking to Maputo approach control and had been asked to report reaching three thousand feet on his decent.

When the co-pilot turned the aircraft he unwittingly entered a South African militarised zone of specially restricted airspace. The nature of the area meant it was under radar surveillance twenty-four hours a day. The flight crew of the Tupolev were unaware of their navigational error but Jacko's boys knew exactly where Samora Machel and his entourage were heading – into a mountain.

The Tupolev brought its forty-four passengers and crew below three thousand feet and the Captain took control for landing. During the last thirty-two seconds of President Samora Machel's life, a ground-proximity warning siren was screaming at the pilots. Yet during those vital last seconds, as they peered through the windscreen searching for runway lights, they may have assumed a power failure at Maputo, a common occurrence. According to the aircraft's black box, the aircraft collided with the Mbuzini hillside at two thousand one hundred and eighty-seven feet. The witness said that was roughly seven hundred feet above where he and other Recces lay in hiding, yet they all felt the impact, and the heat, and later, the guilt, hence his statement.

∞

Waiting for Chios, Andrew and I eventually picked up the conversation and discussed some of the Recce's activities outside of South Africa.

"Andrew, I have no idea how Jacko was funded. There's no publicly sanctioned budget, and murdering people in foreign lands is expensive."

"Very expensive, particularly the Stealth operation you mentioned, who supplied the nerve gas, and where are the bodies?"

"I don't know, maybe there's a mass grave. I do know about the nerve gas, we supplied it."

"We?"

"I have a second report, analysing a chemical and biological warfare programme, Project Costa. There was a government funded programme to produce chemical and biological warfare agents."

Andrew finished his whisky, stuck a hand in the air for a waiter and stared at his empty glass, and then he spoke.

"We researched a defensive-only capability, that was always the line – manufacturing the stuff and actually using it, that's international dynamite."

"Well, we didn't only use it, we also sold it, to Gaddafi, and I think he sold it on to Hussein."

"Fucking Jesus! Libya and Iraq?"

Andrew's voice fell away to a squeak. I offered upturned palms as a gesture of agreement, and disbelief.

"I know, it's unreal." I said.

∞

"Ah, here comes the ANC's answer to the Delphic Oracle."

I looked up to see the exact opposite of a slimy Leviathan. The man walking towards me was tall, elegant, expensively dressed, and exuding poise.

"Good evening Andrew."

Chios cast a glance across the table towards me and smiled.

"Tim, a pleasure to meet you."

After a few pleasantries, we settled unanimously for lentil cream soup and smoked pork, together with a Stellenbosch red.

"What are we here to discuss, Andrew? You were a bit short when you invited me, sent for me." Chios said.

"Joshua, I hope your vocabulary extends to the word shtum, because I would like an explanation as to why you have kept shtum regarding de Klerk's report. You have always denied its existence, and yet, remarkably, a copy of it is here on the table. In answering you should treat me with caution. You are on loan to the Ethics Committee – I am presently your master. If I sense any further lying, I shall give your young judicial arse a rigorous public kicking."

"Pass the wine please, Tim." Chios said.

An obvious tactical delay, an opportunity to think.

"Andrew, you've stitched me up. I've been ambushed. Tim, how did you come by this report?"

"The postman." I said.

"I think I get it. A letter from heaven, from beyond the grave?"

"In a manner of speaking, yes."

"So you have Jacko's copy? Important people have been tearing their hair out trying to ascertain where it went. And others, less important but infinitely more dangerous, have been doing the very same thing. I can tell you, the longer it's in your possession the less likely it is you'll see the month out. I'm surprised you're still alive."

I recognised an opportunity to mention Oscar's demise but didn't.

"Joshua, I want an explanation."

"Andrew, I would not have chosen to lie but I had my instructions. In any event, you're a purveyor of ethics, a philosopher, you believe excruciatingly in forgiveness. I believe in crushing testicles. In the context of the reconciliation process your philosophy is right. I admire you for easing the pain of what happened in this country and for taking us forward through a process of forgiveness. However, when it comes to the Machiavellian shit who authorised, and is personally responsible, for the Recce's atrocities, which I remind you, involved thousands of deaths, then forgiveness is not appropriate, disembowelling tools are."

"I have a duty to publish." I said.

I can remember being annoyed as I spoke, there was an overly self-righteous tone in my voice.

"I have a reason to stop you publishing." Chios said.

"What sort of reason? Maybe like a defoliant compensation claim running into tens of millions?"

"You must receive a lot of information in the post. Dorothy Tutani's constituents have a legitimate claim. We know their accusations are true, but we don't want that information made public at this time, and passing over a small fortune to a bunch of mostly tobacco farmers so they can carry on killing people is not a government priority."

"Joshua, I'm still waiting for an explanation." Andrew said.

"On the face of it we should have nothing to fear from publication, although we do have some anxieties about technological know-how falling into the wrong hands. Also, it all happened before we came to power, and of course in almost every case we blacks were the victims. However, if the report is published it will still be embarrassing – questions will be asked for which we have no answers. The people involved have never been identified, although we know they reported directly to Jacko, which is why, until the bastard did a high dive from the Gourits bridge, we were pinning our hopes on him spilling the beans."

"They were army personnel, reconnaissance commandos, how could you not know their identities?" I said.

"They were moonlighting, moving from an enrolled role to a clandestine one – Jacko assigned them to their duties and he protected their anonymity to maintain secrecy. I had the impression he was definitely ready to trade their names for the right deal. We are vulnerable in other ways, we have no idea how the operations were funded, or any indication as to the paymaster's identity. More depressingly, there were a couple of occasions when chemical and biological warfare agents were deployed. The obvious question will be where did we get them? Unfortunately, in direct contravention of the Non-Proliferation Treaty to which South Africa is a signatory, we manufactured them, using a string of front companies as a facade."

"And here's a surprising connection – one of the front companies was Rainmaker." I said.

"What is your mailman, a fucking magician? So you have Fulsoma's analysis too?" Chios said.

I ignored the question and continued.

"Another reason you want things kept under wraps is because the administration wasn't able to stop the things quickly enough, the momentum was too great. Right?"

"Well, it's mostly stopped now." Chios said.

"Mostly? What the hell's still going on?" Andrew

said.

"There's a huge drug-manufacturing and distribution operation, born out of Project Costa's infrastructure. It's supplying cities and townships with crack cocaine, rocket fuel for violent crime. As well as that, the Americans say our warfare agents are still reaching terrorist organisations and regimes run by madmen."

"Such as Libya and Iraq?" I said.

"We don't want the world to know, not until we've identified the individuals involved, erased any residual activity. I've been told the handful of people we're looking for will know who to take out to stop us getting to them, if you go public with that report. Tim, I want these people for what they've done, and Andrew, I don't want them to testify and walk free, clutching an illuminated immunity scroll with blood stained grubby hands. These people should be tried for their crimes and fucked, not pardoned."

"Joshua. your contribution during the formative period of the Ethics Committee was invaluable, and your incisiveness pointed us in the right direction. Yet you cannot continue to work with me without an unquestionable commitment to the process of forgiveness. Forgiveness is not conditional, and once given it is not rescindable. You have just resigned. I'd be grateful for a written confirmation of your sudden and unexpected departure, something that will bear public scrutiny.

"If that's not to your liking, I'll be only too pleased to do a piece on breakfast TV tomorrow morning, telling the story of how a talented and ambitious junior member of the Department of Justice suppressed evidence vital to the Ethics Committee's functioning. At which point I guess you'll be hung out to dry by your senior colleagues who will deny any knowledge of your maverick foolishness.

"You also need to know that the Ethics Committee will continue in session for another ten days, until Friday 16th, and those who come here to confess their crimes during that period are entitled, if eligible, to a statutory and legally defined immunity.

"I have a responsibility, given me by Parliament, to hear them out and enter them in to the national process of reconciliation. Among the many I still expect to interview, if I come across the individuals you are pursuing, they will be treated with impeccable impartiality and dealt with in exactly the same way as the other racially motivated murderers of the apartheid era who have already confessed.

"Joshua, ongoing criminality is different, and I have no authority in that area. Any amnesty claimants retaining current aspirations in the criminal world are yours, on a plate, to eviscerate at your pleasure."

"How generous." Chios said.

I sat marvelling at Andrew's strength – exculpating some of the worst violators of human rights the world had ever seen, it was an act of profound magnanimity and forgiveness.

The Brothers

Komatipoort Mozambique

At the Komatipoort border crossing Moses climbed down from his cab to find things uneventfully chaotic – lorries were strewn along each side of the road for a good half-mile leading to the checkpoint. The vehicles were temporarily abandoned while their drivers massed in or outside of the customs hall dealing with their triplicate paperwork, which involved a lot of shouting and a conspicuous amount of bribery – or, at least, most palms seemed to be giving or receiving currency.

Entering Mozambique on foot was uncomplicated. There were never any questions asked, bags searched or individuals stopped. It still took time, but it was straightforward enough. That morning there were several hundred people walking towards the border, kicking up dust into the diesel laden air, before joining the long queue that snaked its way to a passport-stamping counter.

Moses stood at the roadside, peering into the crowd as it passed, tracking up and down in search of a familiar face, but by six o'clock there was still no sign of Jabu. There was nothing Moses could do but sit it out and so he climbed back into Constance, reclined his seat and snoozed.

An hour or so later he was woken by the sound of Jabu climbing in beside him. Moses straightened his seatback and sat up, and was shocked.

"Shit, Jabu, that's some ear piercing."

"Brother, don't you mock me."

As Jabu spoke, Moses saw his teeth, or the lack of them.

"Kunjani?" Moses said.

"How am I? Oh yeah, I'm fine, 'cept now I got a mouth like yours and a fucking great hole in my ear, man. What you been doing, Moses?"

"Jabu, I'm sorry, I'm really sorry. I didn't realise

they'd come after me and find you. What's that smell?"

"I couldn't help it." Jabu said.

"Help what?"

"Pissing my pants."

"Jesus, Jabu."

"Moses, stop fucking laughing and pass me some trousers."

"I don't have any spare trousers."

"Shorts, then."

"I don't have any shorts, Jabu. What are you on?"

"What you got in that bulging Nike bag then?"

"Ah, take a look."

Jabu bent down and unzipped the kitbag. There was a long stillness.

"Fucker. How much you got there, Moses?"

"We, brother, we. We got millions."

"What the fuck has you done?"

"I had a little bump. When the mess was cleared up I found it lying in the road under the cab."

"What sort of mess? Anybody hurt?"

"Jabu, I just nudged a parked Mercedes, it was nothing."

"Moses, if you just nudged it, what d'you mean, mess?"

"There were some clothes, and things, lying around."

"Clothes? Whose clothes?"

"The driver's. The driver of the Mercedes. Jabu, he was naked, the driver. Took his clothes off and scattered them around. He was naked, face down on the bonnet of the car."

"Naked? So, you wonder over, pat his arse, take his money, say thanks and drive on?"

"No, I didn't talk to him at all. By the time I'd climbed down from the cab he was gone."

"Gone?"

"Jabu, I didn't mean to, but I killed him."

"You KILLED HIM! For money!"

"No, not for money."

"For KICKS?"

"Jabu, fuck fooling around. Listen, it wasn't just

anybody, it was General Jacko Jackson."

"Jacko? Maggot, hyena-shit, fuck-face, Jacko? Recce Jacko?"

"That'll be him."

"Was it his money?"

"Suppose."

"Brother, you's a fucking genius! Moses, when people finds out, you's a township hero. How d'you kill him."

"Bumped his car off the Gourits' Bridge."

"Wowee, that's a long way down. Moses, that white thing that pierced my ear, broke my teeth, what it wanted, 'part from a chance to blow your brains away, was an attaché case. D'you find this money in a case?"

"Yeah, with some documents I sent to the newspapers. Jabu let's get into Mozambique, and have a beer on Jacko."

∞

The brothers snaked back and forth in the queue, heading towards the stamping counter. Moses told Jabu what had happened and Jabu told Moses what had happened. After forty-five minutes snaking, and some strange looks as people caught a whiff of the bacterial colony thriving on Jabu's involuntary emission, they were stamped and through, standing in the Mozambique sunshine, smiling toothlessly at each other.

Twenty minutes later, huddled together on a bus bound for Maputo, they had a whispered conversation.

"So, what we gonna do, Moses?"

"Get away, far as possible. Remember Pete Mashaba? He's still a waiter at that fishing lodge on Bazaruto. It's out of the way up there. Pete can help us, somewhere to stay while we think."

"Okay, but a couple of nights in Maputo, yeah? I can get to fix my ear, maybe my teeth."

Roli & Milton

Bazaruto Mozambique

Three days later Moses and Jabu reached Vilanculos, a small coastal town northeast of Maputo, populated by fishermen and their families and a few thousand palm trees. They took a boat from the tranquil fishing harbour to the main island of the Bazaruto Archipelago, a string of tiny tropical Edens, strewn like sand from a giant's hand through five hundred miles of azure serenity in the shallows of the Indian Ocean. It was a two hour journey during which the brothers could finally relax, leaving the mainland behind enroute to their hideaway.

"Jabu, your ear's not so bad. The doc did a good job, bit heavy on the Mercurochrome, looks a little, ah, tandooried."

"Moses, fuck off."

"How's the tooth varnish?"

"It's stopped the pain. Moses, why don't we just check in as guests at the Bazaruto Lodge? We got the money."

"It's 'cos we got the money we can't. We need to lay low. Guests hand over passports. I'd prefer to be anonymous, or somebody else, not me. In fact I feel a change coming on – yes, I am now, Godfrey Redboroko, and Jabu, you, yous Abraham Redboroko."

"Do I look like an Abraham? You wanna change my name, call me Milton."

∞

The reception area in the Bazaruto Lodge was intimidatingly quiet, and posh. Moses parked his luggage, which like Jabu's, contained millions of dollars, cleared his throat and began a conversation with female receptionist.

"I wonder can you help us? We're friends of Pete Mashaba, and..."

The receptionist's eyes sparkled, she opened her face with a wide smile and spoke before Moses had finished.

"Of course, but I'm sure we weren't expecting you

until next week. Are you Milton Khumalo?"

Before Moses could sort the confusion, Jabu, unable to believe his ears, stepped forward and put one hand on his brother's shoulder and stretched out the other towards the receptionist.

"No, I'm Milton." He said.

"Hi Milton, I'm Naomi Soni, and you must be?"

Naomi was pointing her finger at Moses.

"Naomi, you know better than I do who I am. Go on, tell me." Moses said.

"Roli Khumalo, I assume." Naomi said.

"That's right." Jabu said.

"What else do you know about us?" Moses said.

"According to Peter, you're both great waiters and you're reliable. It's why he recommended you both once he knew he was off to work at Sun City.

"What happened to your ear, Milton?" Naomi said.

"Hyena, that's partly why we's a week early. Hoped you might let us take our accommodation and relax, try to forget the hyena attack, before starting next week."

"Yeah? I'll ask the manager."

Naomi dialled an extension and after a brief conversation replaced the receiver.

He says fine. I'll take you over."

∞

They left the reception area along a raised wood-decked walkway, dappled in the shade of swaying beech trees and suspended three metres above the loamy soil. The walkway led in a straight to the workers' accommodation, and Roli and Milton followed Naomi in an excited silence, throwing glances back and forth, in cahoots with each other. They passed the restaurant, the swimming pool, and the bar, enroute to their lodgings.

"The guest accommodation surrounds the pool area here. There are twelve chalets. We're presently fully booked, mostly with South Africans, but we do have people from the UK and Japan, and we have a honeymoon couple.

"I assume you'd like to share with each other, rather than with strangers, and so you're in here. We trust the lodge people, but the villagers occasionally creep in unnoticed. So, if you have any valuables, keep them in the safe at reception. I'll send Gladstone over to say hello, he's our caretaker-cum-night watchman, and he'll give you a tour of the lodge and its facilities. Welcome to Bazaruto."

"Thanks, Naomi." Roli and Milton said, in unison.

Moses pushed open the door to their rondavel and stepped inside, followed by Milton who was walking backwards with his eyes fixed on Naomi rocking hips.

"Jabu?"

"Milton," Jabu said.

"Milton, we'll have to take turns, looking after the money. We can't put it in the safe, and we can't leave it here for the villagers to carry away."

"Roli, don't be mad. We can't let the stuff rule our lives. We just bury it, keep a roll, hide the rest. We can dig a hole or two, put the money in and cover it over. Maybe get some rush matting, pin it to the ground over the holes, lay the bedrolls on top. Done."

"Okay. Let's do it," Moses said.

In the soft soil it was easy to bury their money. All but a handful of the dosh was in the ground in no time, and they were lying on their backs staring at the thatched roof when they heard a croaky, questioning voice.

"Hello?"

"Hello" Moses said.

"Hello, I'm Gladstone, Naomi sent me."

Gladstone was on the far side of seventy, with a banana shaped spine, and yellowish skin that was stretched in odd places by his protruding bones. The three of them walked back towards the pool, with Gladstone croaking a mix of superfluous and useful information. He said he had never left the island, but he was certain the whole country took a dive after the colonials pulled out.

"What's the point, running your own country, if it's trash?" Gladstone said.

He didn't wait for an answer, he simply went on, the right-hand fridge behind the bar was dodgy and produced warm beer. The Tanzanian washer up was available and he'd do it for fifty cents. The couple in number eleven were on honeymoon, and did Roli or Milton have any smokes?

∞

Inside chalet eleven, Emma and Stefan were continuing a conversation they had started a few days earlier.

"Grim stuff, that's all I've ever heard. Now, though, I need to know. So, what happened?" Emma said.

"In the beginning I thought we were justified, but..."

"Go on, Stefan."

"I left the military with parts of my life shut down, roped off."

"As a way of coping?"

"Yeah, I suppose, a way of forgetting. I tidied things, packed them away, roped them off."

"Andrew is offering a chance for you to tell him what's roped off.'

"It would be dangerous for me to testify at the Truth and Reconciliation hearings. I was near the top, above me was Theo, and between him and Jacko, just one other."

"Who was that?"

"I don't know. He was known as the Boss-man. Maybe the others got to know him, later, after I had left."

"Stefan, tell me about the grim stuff. What happened?"

"Murder, but on a huge scale. Kassinga, where I saved the Theo's life, it was a nightmare. Intelligence got everything wrong. We attacked what we thought was a terrorist encampment, turned out to be a refugee camp packed with women and children.

A few months later we took on a hundred-plus terrorists, and tested a chemical warfare agent on them. We spread ourselves out upwind of their encampment wearing gas masks, ironically we were laying in an exquisite and beautiful wilderness, just north of the Kunene River in Angola, deep into the vast grassy plain.

"I remember scrabbling around on my belly, inching over the vegetation, in fear of the unassigned death that clung to the whole savannah.

"A couple of choppers released a peppermint-coloured cloud of vapour that moved down wind and overwhelmed the terrorists, paralysing them as it settled in their lungs. Around the washrooms they lay face down in the dirt, shaving cream on their faces, and others were slumped in the makeshift latrines. In the field kitchen an unlucky cook had gone down head first into boiling oil."

"Oh Jesus, Stefan."

"I know. Grotesque. Twenty or so guards lay dead in their bunks, one with his open eyes fixed on a picture of his girlfriend, green slime oozing from his mouth. There was a complete platoon crooked-rigid in camouflage gear, lying flat in the grass, rifles slung over their shoulders and unused grenades hanging from their hip belts.

"Yet their commander, Colonel Raimondo de Baptista, not that we knew it immediately, he was still alive, thanks to a damp cloth soaked in water, that he held close to his face. We soon realised there were others, entirely paralysed but breathing. I was with Theo when he talked to HQ – all hell broke loose over the radio, and after a lot of swearing he was told that two Chinooks were on the way and to chuck every last one of them in the Atlantic."

"No! Even the ones that were alive?"

"Yeah. I told the Theo I wouldn't do it. He said I had to, or I could personally shoot each one of them between the eyes and make a hell of a mess. I still refused – that was the end for me, I just walked off into the bush. When the Chinooks landed Smit came to fetch me, and as he came close I amazed myself. I unholstered my gun and, well, I shot myself through the thigh."

"Stefan? Christ Almighty!"

"The medics were quick to reach me, and they applied a tourniquet, lay me on a stretcher and were carrying me away by the time the Theo arrived. He called me a stupid bastard, yet I think he had doubts himself.

"And that was it. I was out."

"Emma, the army really screwed my life. I have nightmarish recalls, from Kassinga and the refugee camp. The memories are right here with me. Mothers to be, with their wombs split open like popped corn, and the low-level whimpering of writhing half-life, moving to death, hundreds of them, burst and leaking, spread like puce silage over the bright green grass."

"Stefan, go see Andrew, but soon, he's winding things up."

Raimondo de Baptista's Last Moments

A Few Hundred Feet Above the Atlantic

Miguel Lopes is fifty eight years old. He still lives in Baia dos Tigres and still walks with a limp, from an injury he received while fishing the same day that Stefan Taylor shot himself through the thigh.

On that day, just prior to Miguel's sixteenth birthday, he rose early and set off to go fishing with his father and his cousin, in their family's small, blue painted clinker built boat. The boat's clinker construction was a cultural boat-building hand-me-down from the Portuguese, colonial occupiers of Miguel's homeland, Angola. Other fishermen from the village set off also, forming a small flotilla of some eleven boats, and they all chugged gently together towards the open ocean, joking, laughing and speculating about the day's catch.

They moved forward under a low level, grey layer of nimbostratus cloud, thick with potential rain. All the fishermen knew the cloud contained rain, and they sensed it was a short matter of time before they felt it on their skin.

Yet none of them could have anticipated the type of rain that would fall, or the death and destruction it would bring with it – how could they have done?

According to Miguel's later statements, the morning was misty and the air slightly moist, but there was no wind, no white horses. There was a collective splutter of smoky exhausts, happening quietly across the flat, ripple-less water – even as they moved forward there was a stillness. The cloud base was barely above Miguel's head, and there was an occasional whale spout as the flotilla manoeuvred slowly in the haze through a small pod.

Several thousand feet above that tranquillity, Colonel Raimondo de Baptista had found the strength to reach up and remove Theo's leg knife from its sheaf and plunge the eight-inch steel blade through his enemy's leg. Cuba's local hero held on with two hands and let his own weight pull the sharp cutting edge down through the length of Theo's quadriceps to the knee.

A handful of soldiers were on him in an instant but they couldn't release Baptista's grip on the handle, and so they pulled the blade from Theo's leg and threw Baptista from their Chinook still clutching the knife. The colonel was followed by sixty or so of his soldiers, some dead, some paralysed and near to death, all thrown or kicked from the choppers.

The human rain that fell that morning caught the fishermen of Baia dos Tigres totally off guard. The floppy, twisting, almost dancing Cuban bodies, hurtling through the cloud at over 140 miles an hour, pulverised the boats and the fishermen. Seventeen villagers were killed, including Miguel's father, who died instantly right in front of him, accompanied by the splintering crunch of his bones as the soldier's body crushed him to death.

During those moments Miguel sat shaking in the boat, wondering why God's hand had covered him, and not his father, or his cousin, both of whom died that day.

Dorothy Tutani & Joshua Chios

Cape Town

Dorothy Tutani's office was stylish and welcoming, with a beaming Mandela looking down on us from the wall, and Desmond and the children were smiling from a framed picture on her desk. While Dorothy poured herbal tea from a metal pot painted with animal motifs, I began to tell her what I knew about Rainmaker.

"That's the background, Dorothy. What can you tell me?"

"Well, if you're saying that Chios agrees with us in private, then everything we've said all along is right. Rainmaker did have a product capable of making rain, but that's not what they were testing at Easthope. They were testing the capabilities of a virulent defoliant, and as it happened it worked shockingly well. Tim, did you know that Stefan Taylor was involved with Rainmaker?"

"Stefan? No."

"Yeah, he set the whole thing up, that's when Stefan and Emma met. At the time he gave Marty Schwartz a lot of work, ferrying military people and potential buyers around in his chopper, producing aerial surveys and showing off the havoc they'd wreaked in the fields."

"Dorothy, why did the Government want a defoliant? What did they do with it?"

"I've not been able to find out. There's a rumour says they never used it in this country but that it was exported."

"Any ideas?"

"Not really. I read one heavily redacted memo suggesting Russia, but I thought, that's ridiculous. We were effectively at war with them during those years, when they were arming and financially supporting Angola and

Mozambique."

"Any mention of Libya?"

"You kidding me? What makes you say that?"

"I received some sensitive information, anonymously, in the post. It was all about a secretive chemical and biological warfare programme. There was the suggestion of a Libyan connection, and Rainmaker was listed as a company fronting the programme. From the way you've described the damage the defoliant caused it would be reasonable to think of it as a weapon."

"Okay, so it's not a defoliant, it's a chemical warfare agent, manufactured in contravention of the international non-proliferation agreement, of which South Africa is a signatory. What a bunch of bastards we had running this country. No wonder Chios is trying to keep it quiet."

"Incidentally, he rang me this morning, wants to have a chat before I fly back."

"You could take a message – tell him I have a close friend who's received a report from an anonymous source. Tell him it substantiates my constituents' claims but I would be loathed to make the information in it public because it's not in the Government's interest. Say I hope not to be placed in an invidious position, and tell him I look forward to his proposals for settlement."

"Talking of messages, Rosy said to say hello."

"Thanks, it was good to see her at the wedding. I was surprised that she wants to get out of banking, and is even thinking of returning to South Africa."

"Really, I didn't know."

"Yes, she wants to do something socially worthwhile, expressed an interest in my housing project. Not that she'll be able to do much without funding. She wasn't sure about coming alone."

"What do you mean?"

"She was telling me about her man in London."

"Oh, I didn't know that, either. First I've heard of him."

"He's a banker."

∞

I was preoccupied leaving Dorothy's office – the thought of two poncy bankers was a difficult concept, and somehow far more important than a non-proliferation agreement. Joshua's room, just down the corridor, with its oak panelling and leather seats, was a grander setting but somehow, cold, unwelcoming.

"Tim, I'm not prepared to have these people pardoned. We're looking at a bunch of unfeeling white supremacist racists who murdered thousands of innocent blacks, men, women and children."

"They weren't all black." I said.

"Quite right. I apologise, but they were overwhelmingly black, and their murderers should stand trial, not be put out to grass laughing.

Tim, some people use just means as a defence, you know how it goes – they did what they did believing their actions were justified. But the people I want, they had no justification for what they did. They know within themselves they were wrong, every murdering inch of the way."

"What have you got in mind?"

"We know who was in charge, and most likely he was not the victim of a road traffic accident last weekend. Most likely he was bumped off."

"The bridge?"

"Very funny, but yes. Look, he was about to shit on the very people I want, and I'll tell you, that makes me think they're close."

"They tried to kill me. Bloody nearly succeeded."

"What? When?"

"Yesterday, blew my plane to smithereens."

"Jesus. Tim, why would they do that?"

"Presumably, they think I can incriminate them."

"No, you're missing the point."

"I am?"

"Yes, I thought you were an investigative journalist."

"Joshua, WHAT point am I missing?"

"How would they know you even had the information to incriminate them? You only received the reports 48 hours ago, and they tried to trash you yesterday."

"Fuck."

"Somebody on my list is close to you. Too close, it

seems, and if they've tried once."

"Fuck."

"Tim, you want the story. I want the people."

"You mean I want the story, and you want me as bait?"

"Possibly, but let's see what else we can unearth."

"Joshua, you're aware that I'm a friend of Dorothy Tutani. Earlier this morning she told me that a friend, she wouldn't say who, had shown her a secret report, and apparently it supports the claims for damages of her constituency farmers. Dorothy wanted me to convey to you her hope that pursuing the report's publication, in order to reach a settlement, would not be necessary."

Joshua eyed me with a bored resignation.

"Is that so. Tell Dorothy I'll be in touch. Tim, thanks for making the effort to fly down. It was good to talk. Have a good flight back to Jozi."

Billy Saves My Life

In The Air

Towards the end of my return flight to Jozi we began our decent to the runway and levelled off, at around the same height as an enormous white pelican. Billy had made good progress in four days, and was flying just ahead of us, but at several hundred miles an hour slower. Ten minutes later when the illuminated seatbelt sign went on with a ding, I opened my eyes and looked about me, smiling at the passenger in the next seat. My fellow traveller was a thick-set muscular type, subconsciously twirling an ornate fountain pen, attempting to solve crossword clues. The answer to five down jumped out of the page at me, which was lying flat across the adjacent fold down table, and then eleven down, both easy cryptics. I decided to strike up a conversation and talk about the answers, but in that instant I was thrown forcefully to one side, and with a violence that caused the half-drunk sparkling water I was holding to be throwed over my shocked neighbour.

The gush of cold effervescent across his facial skin produced a jerked reflex reaction that shot down his right arm and applied pressure to the fountain pen's cap end – which I later learnt was its trigger. The Airbus took such a lurch that being thrown over my fellow passenger forced his arm and pen first sideways and then forwards, where its activated telescopic syringe punctured the forward seat's upholstery. As the aircraft stabilised the forward seat's occupant fell backwards onto the needle's sharpness, and the protruding point released a nerve agent into her spine, before snapping unnoticed beneath the tissues of her flesh.

"Ladies and Gentlemen, this is your captain speaking, please accept my apologies. I do hope nobody was injured during that emergency procedure. If you need assistance please press the call button in your overhead console. The good news is that we've just avoided a major bird strike that would have had dire consequences. We've just flown around the most enormous pelican I have ever seen. Thank you."

"You're drenched, I'm so sorry. Tim Kitson." I said.

"These things happen. Gary Roper."

"At least I managed to miss your crossword. Gary, I've done a couple of the clues."

"I don't have a pen, the barrel snapped, being thrown around."

I pulled out a Biro and shrugged at its cheapness.

"Are you travelling on business, Tim?"

"I'm on the way home. And you?"

"Eco-tourism. I'm after a connecting flight to Vilanculos, to check out an offshore destination."

"Fabulous part of the world. Look, five down – two fools taken in to become a murderer. Get it?"

"I don't really, Tim."

"Assassin." I said.

Roper turned very slowly, looking into my eyes, seemingly in an attempt to assess the word as he pronounced it.

"Assassin?"

"Yes, look. Two fools, well a fool is an ass, so that's 'ass' 'ass'. And the second ass has taken the word 'in', and placed it on the end. So, ass, ass, in, assassin. How about fourteen across? Racist hit parade, nine letters." I said.

"So, while I'm sitting on the beach tomorrow, you'll be slogging it out in Jozi." He said.

"I'll be cocooned in my glass tower at the Johannesburg Post; I'm a reporter. Apartheid."

"What?"

"Fourteen across, it's an anagram, of hit parade, with a connection to racism. So, apartheid, assassin, that should keep you going." I said.

Of course, I had no idea of the irony, nor at the time did I realise that Billy had saved my life, yet at the expense of another. The lady immediately in front of Roper, according to my colleague's reporting the following day, was Rosemary Windsor from Ontario. Prior to landing a steward hovered in the aisle sympathising with her complaint that she found it difficult to breathe. The steward repositioned the air nozzle to blow directly over her mouth, and then smiled in my direction. The young businesswoman from Canada pressed the call button a further two times before the airbus taxied to a stop, at which point the steward returned to find Rosemary Windsor dead in a pool of her own urine, shortly after the contents of Roper's pen had overwhelmed her central nervous system.

What A Charlie

London

Rosy pushed open the door to her London apartment, abandoned her bags in the hallway and paced through to the kitchen's ringing phone.

"Hello."

"You made it."

"Hi, I just walked through the door."

"Good journey?"

"Compared with yesterday and flying to the dam it was a dream. At least nobody tried to kill me, although the in-flight catering came menacingly close. How are you?"

"Fine, I just rang to say hello and, well… I wanted to say how much I enjoyed seeing you."

"That's nice. Tim, thanks. Hey, I didn't sleep much during the flight, gave me a chance to mulch the brain. It's time I came home."

"I can imagine, getting back with a busy workload must be a pain in the arse."

"I don't mean here, it's time I came home to South Africa. I decided finally just north of Marrakech, as I was slipping off the continent."

"Dorothy mentioned you were thinking of coming back. That would be wonderful. What would you do?"

"Haven't a clue, really. I'm interested in Dorothy's work, I don't mean politically but socially, housing for instance. I'm no longer interested in banking. Fact is, I can't wait to hand in my notice and walk."

"Rosy, if you want something temporary, come home and help me track down the baddies from Project Costa."

"Tell you what I was thinking last night, entranced by the wing tip strobe. I reckon your dad's on to something, when you find the baddies you'll find the pot of gold that funded them."

"Apart from my old man you're the only one to have mentioned money, but then you're a banker. So, how about it? Come home and help me."

"I might just do that. I'll think it through. I'll go now, a shower and a sleep is needed. Thanks for ringing."

"It's good to talk. I'll call again in the morning."

∞

"Rosy slept for three hours after our chat, but by late morning she had arrived for lunch at a sushi bar in Covent Garden. Charlie, her banker boyfriend, who had never, I learnt later, been bound for Shug's matrimonial jacaranda, seemed more interested in his food, Rosy said, than in what she was telling him about their future.

"Try the salmon nigiri, it's fantastic."

"Charlie, can you hear a word of what I'm saying to you? I am going to live in South Africa?"

"What will you do?" Charlie said.

"I don't know, something worthwhile. Does that matter?"

"What's the rush?"

"I just feel as if I have to go. I'm sorry. Charlie, if you need some time to think things through."

"Actually, the tuna maki is amazing."

It wasn't until Rosy began perspiring in response to the Thai fishcakes that Charlie's attitude really got to her, a stupid boyish defence mechanism she decided.

By the time lunch was over they were holding hands across the black granite tabletop wishing one another luck for the future.

"I don't suppose you want to come back for the holiday we've booked? I've already paid. No, of course not." Charlie said.

Leaving the restaurant, Rosy waved goodbye from the back seat of her cab and headed off to Gunnersbury Self Storage, via Trafalgar Square and the South African embassy, where she had attended countless demonstrations during her time at the LSE, campaigning for Mandela's release, selling T-shirts and button badges to spread the word.

The cab left Trafalgar Square via the Mall towards Buckingham Palace, home of the British monarchy, which had failed to endear itself to Rosy, whose personal world resonated with the correction of injustice, and not the perpetuation of advantage. There was also the nonpicturesque notion of the future king's aspirations to be reincarnated as a tampon inside Camilla – how even could anyone say that, totally bonkers. For a brief moment Rosy had a flash back to the single dark line and the words *not pregnant* from the testing kit she had used earlier in the day, and she re-experienced a profound relief.

At Chiswick roundabout the cab took the last exit and five minutes later pulled up at the entrance to Gunnersbury Self Storage.

"I'll be ten minutes, then I want to go to the Barbican." Rosy said.

The cabbie nodded and Rosy entered the depository. When she first arrived from the USA, temporary accommodation made the self-storage unit essential, but she kept it on, filling it with odds and sods, stuff she wanted to keep but didn't want in her daily space, including the archived paperwork from the trading floor at the Chicago Commodity Exchange, which she began reading travelling home to the Barbican.

Towards the end of the afternoon Rosy rang Toby in America, but only to be disappointed with a recorded message, relaying a mobile number, which she also rang. The second recorded message was also disappointing, but she asked for him to return her call, saying she wanted to pick his brains on the period they helped Al Calascione.

∞

Rosy produced a wheel-cum-space-station sketch of the bullion crisis. The rim comprised various country names, bent slightly to the circle's arc. The spokes had alternating arrowheads to represent the flow of gold from the periphery to the hub and back again, or put another way, from the periphery to the Chicago Commodity Exchange and back again. And dotted around the page were various dollar signs and values. When her phone rang she was considering a large question mark drawn to the right of Russia.

"Rosy, Toby Weinberg. You must be psychic. I was about to ring you when I received your message. I'm in London for a few days, over at the Lloyds building, comparing notes on the proceeds of crime."

"Really! Will I get to see you? Have you got free

time?"

"How about tomorrow morning, I'm free 'til eleven thirty."

"Oh, fantastic. Yes, the morning's fine."

∞

"Tim, is that you?"

"Morning Rosy. How is it?"

"Pretty well. It's a strange line. Where the hell are you?"

"In the bush at Gravelotte, I came down last night. It's a satellite phone, no cellular network out here."

"What are you doing in the bush? You've a story to write."

"I'm writing it, and there's more chance of it getting finished here – somebody took another pop at me."

"God, no. What happened?"

"The poisoned pen routine."

"Are you okay?"

"Yeah, I'm fine, but they're obviously capable of tracking me, and unfortunately a young Canadian woman died instead of me."

"Christ, Tim."

"The poison meant for me was accidentally syringed into her back, poor woman. So, I'm in the bush, thought I'd lie low for a while, finish reading the reports and write up the story here, far from the reach of racist psychopaths."

"OK, but be careful because we are really on to something. I'm expecting Toby Weinberg around any minute to discuss South Africa's involvement in the bullion crisis – everything, all the stuff we discussed, it's stacking up, and it's big. Actually, it's fantastamagorically fucking enormous! And there's other stuff we haven't discussed, just as important, it's all part of the same scene.

"Tim, come and lie low in London, better night life than the bush, and there's a lot I need to tell you. How about it?"

"Rosy, yesterday I asked you to come home and help me here."

"I will if you will. There's stuff to do here first."

"I'm at least six hours from anywhere. I had to drive

here."

"You mean you're only six hours from Jozi. You can easily catch tonight's flight if they have a seat. I'll check it out and ring you back."

I knew it was a great idea, but wanted to square it with Bruce. I began throwing things together, waiting on Rosy's call back, speculating on what she may have discovered.

"Tim, I've booked you a seat on the eight thirty flight this evening. All they had was Upper Class."

"For Christ's sake! Rosy, I can't afford Upper Class."

"You won't have to, I've paid."

"Really? Thanks. I'm not sure what to tell Bruce."

"He knows you're in the bush, putting together the scoop of the year. He can reach you any time by satellite phone, which doubtless he'll do at some point, but, BUT – satellite telephones are geographically anonymous. You could be back in Jozi any time after Monday morning, I wouldn't tell Bruce a thing. However, if you want to come to Washington on Tuesday, you should probably let him know what you're up to, but not necessarily."

"Washington?"

"I'll pick you up at Heathrow in the morning."

∞

Toby pitched up at Rosy's apartment shortly after she and I had finished talking. Rosy poured some coffee and they sat together overlooking the river and the city ant life below. After the briefest of hellos and niceties Rosy was off in pursuit of the baddies.

"Let's start with the Russians."

"Nice to see you too, Rosy. Okay, first things first. Why do you want to pick my brains? I can't imagine a single good reason, given the aging and decaying state of my head. Sounds almost ghoulish. What's occurring?"

"I'm trying to make a connection, between a bunch of thugs still roaming the streets and what happened in the bullion crisis, when South Africa traded on the Chicago Commodity Exchange during the time we worked there together. I know it was mostly a Russia-America thing about the price of wheat and the value of gold but I remember there was a South African intervention of some sort."

"Okay, but officially I shouldn't be talking with you, so be discreet. I don't think the Russians had a hidden agenda. It was simply coincidence their harvest failed the very same year the Americans had their best wheat crop in half a century."

"Down to El Nino, apparently," Rosy said.

"Yes, and some. I'll come to that in a moment. So, when the Russians raided the Chicago Commodity Exchange to buy up huge quantities of wheat, the price was incredibly low due to that bumper harvest in America. The fact that Russia could buy wheat so cheaply pissed everybody from the White House to the Farmer's Union, and particularly Al Calascione at the US treasury.

Calascione had been waiting months for the right opportunity to smash the gold price and replace it as the currency of last resort with the US dollar, and you know most of that story. That's exactly what he did, fucked the gold price completely, brought the value down from $240 to just over $100 an ounce. For the Russians, who needed to pay for wheat purchases by buying US dollars with gold, it was a disaster, overnight the wheat doubled in price, and Calascione delivered his coup de grace – on the international exchange markets the dollar replaced gold as the go-to currency of last resort."

"I remember," Rosy said, tapping her notebook with a fingertip.

"A Commodity Exchange notebook?"

"Yes. And it says there was a blip in the value of gold during August, back to $184 an ounce, and that's when you told me about the rumours of the South African military trading directly."

"Ah, well since then I've been given security clearance at a higher level, and I can tell you, it wasn't just the military trading, they did it in cahoots with the South African Government. You remember South Africa stopped all gold production, reducing supply, and that's what drove the value back to $184, but within three days they were smelting it again by the mountain load."

"Yes, the intervention seemed futile."

"Well, they held the price high for long enough, and resumed production after the military sold its last tranche of gold. Guess how much they sold?"

"A few tons I expect, I don't know, five, seven tons."

"Three hundred tons."

"Three hundred! They can't have sold three hundred."

"Why not?"

And after a moment's hesitation, looking straight into Toby's eyes, Rosy answered.

"That would have been worth around $2 billion."

"Exactly, which is why that transaction is still an unclosed case. The proceeds were transferred to an account in the British Virgin Islands, and because at the time the transaction was enormously helpful to Al Calascione's campaign to reduce the value of gold, basically a case of oversupply, well, dumping in the market, the US authorities turned a blind eye to the transaction and actively helped cover up the size of the disposal."

"Christ! Toby, where did they get three hundred tons of gold from in the first place?"

"It seems the military were active in the market, buying and selling profitably for a couple of years prior to that August, but that wouldn't explain it all.

"Rosy, I couldn't have this conversation over the telephone, it's a stroke of luck I'm in London."

"Thanks Toby. Do we know who received the money?"

"No, but that doesn't mean we can't try to find out. Don't misunderstand me, it might be impossible, but the money looks to me exactly like the proceeds of crime, and that's precisely the type of money I'm currently chasing."

"So, who do you work for these days?"

"I work for the Government."

"I know that, which begs the question, who do you work for these days?"

"I work in the economics unit of Central Intelligence. My speciality is tracking illicit funds, dirty money used by organised crime and terrorists."

"Impressive."

"Another thing, you mentioned the El Nino damage to the Russian wheat crop. There's an MP here in London, Jim Trebor, he's a colleague of mine and he has a very different version of the failed harvest story. Jim was in

Moscow when it happened. He's a nice guy, go and see him. Here's a contact number and I'll let him know to expect to hear from you. Anyway, I need to get going. I'm presenting a seminar in forty-five minutes."

"Proceeds of crime?"

"Yes, the identification of illicit funds in international markets."

"How do you do that?"

"With difficulty, but laundered money, for instance, often sits in low-interest deposit accounts doing nothing. Ironically the criminals think they'll draw attention to themselves if they move it around too much. Obviously, when they have a specific project to finance they'll draw down the funds, but the rest of the time it just sits there. So any large amounts of money that we track to a standstill immediately arouse our suspicions. If it were clean the owners would be moving the money around to get the best deal.

"Rosy, there's a whole load of intelligence on our computers in Washington. You know, bullion dealing, offshore accounts, that sort of stuff. I can't send it anywhere, but if you want to come over, I can get clearance for you to trawl it."

"Thanks Toby, that's really helpful."

"One last thing, there's another angle to this that nobody understands, and it's possibly the connection you're looking to uncover. When we tracked the timeline of the military's trading we discovered a very interesting crossover. The Russian government sold a one-off consignment of bullion worth $25m, but the proceeds were transferred directly to the very same account used by the military to deposit their sale proceeds."

"What are we saying?"

"That's the thing, I don't know, but there's a connection. Hard to imagine Russians helping South Africans, back then they were effectively at war."

"Yet they paid money into an account used by the military. Toby, the Russians paid $25m, what for, what did they buy?"

An Old-fashioned Apparatchik

Omsk

An answer to Rosy's question could be found four thousand miles to the east of London, alongside the Irtysh River in the city of Omsk, deep into the vast Russian region of Siberia. Vitali Legachev, the old-fashioned apparatchik who had authorised the $25m transfer, was as pained the day Rosy spoke of it as ever he had been. Back in the day, Vitali had made a mistake, and Russia had suffered, big time. Even heading towards his twilight years, revenge for Vitali was an obsessive preoccupation, a permanent blot on his mental landscape that required excision.

When Toby left Rosy for his seminar that morning, in Omsk it was just past nine in the evening. It was black and cold but not entirely still – white flakes from a mild snow fall were swirling around in a quiet chaos over the city rooflines. In the suburb of Irtysh, behind the thickly embroidered curtains of their ground floor apartment in Brezhnev Square, Vitali, together with Nadia and their son, Nikolay, were chewing the political cud.

"The Rainmaker guy, do you still need to get him?" Nikolay said.

"I've got him."

"What do you mean?"

"I had to wait for the blacks to take over in South Africa, a Russian to them is always a friend. There's a black Government and the Communist Party is unbanned. A few weeks and I'll go."

"You can't fly around the world murdering people, those days are gone." Nadia said.

"I'm not going to murder him. I'm going to execute him. Even before Gorbachev came to power I was given the authority, and it's never been revoked."

"Father, you're an old man."

"My body's good, Nikolay. Look at Mandela. He's

fit enough. Anyway, he won't be expecting me."

"Who won't? You're not even sure of his identity." Nadia said.

"I know who he is. The last conversation I had with Reuben Shavit he confirmed it."

"You mean the last conversation Reuben Shavit was allowed to have, he confirmed it." Nadia said.

"Same thing." Vitali said.

Nadia pushed up from the armchair and shuffled off to the kitchen, staring at the floor, sighing in frustration, sad at the inevitable.

"Nikolay, he destroyed communism, hard to imagine but Rainmaker's guy did that, spraying his defoliant through our wheat fields crippled the country."

"Father, we never had communism. Marx was a sociologist not a politician, and what he had in mind never happened here. Marx said you could never have communism before reaching a point of developed socialism. In Russia we never did that either, our country was more repressive than South Africa's apartheid regime. Stalin murdered millions – he stole grain from the peasants, and starving Ukrainians ended up eating each other."

"I forget you made an academic career out of Marx. So what did he do, the man with the poisoned rain?"

"He gave us another chance. After we have sold all of us to all of us, and the planet's unique resource has been exchanged for a world of unsustainable pelf, we will be given a new opportunity to ensure that each person contributes to and receives from society according to their ability and needs.

"Excuse me, by then, as Marx also said, people will have been denied their basic creative instincts to the extent that they'll emerge onto the beachhead of freedom as crippled monstrosities. Son, thousands of people starved to death when the harvest failed."

"Father, what you're after is revenge. Mandela's not about revenge, although God knows he'd have every reason, and Mandela's not going to wipe out the whites like Stalin wiped out the Kulaks. In fact, his Government intends to forgive the white supremacists."

"Nikolay, the man I'm after will be forgiven over my

dead body. And what about the Soviets set adrift, those lost to the capitalist world?"

"We will take them back. After Gorbachev we will take them back, the Baltic states, Crimea, Ukraine. We will bring them home.

∞

In spite of Vitali's protestations and claims of safety, a positive identification nailed him the moment he entered South Africa, which is when Gillmor buzzed Theo Mason sitting two floors above him.

"What can I do for you?" Theo said.

"I've just finished an entry-visa scan, looking for the fucking cartel goons muscling in on our trade, in that respect I didn't find much. But, Theo, I did find a name, it was on our database and so capture automatically."

"Who is it?"

"Vitali Legachev, arrived in the Cape yesterday."

"Legachev, well, well. I'm surprised he's still alive. I know he took out Primakov and Shavit – he's presumably here for us. Find Smit and come up, and send a chopper up to look around, especially over the kop, we're vulnerable from there."

∞

"What can you see?" Theo said.

"Very little." The chopper pilot said. "There's a bunch of hikers heading towards the overnight hut and another lot walking through the valley. I've got a problem with the infrared. There's a quirky temperature convergence, the ground's temporarily radiating body temperature in the shade. There are some acacia I can't immediately interrogate, but one of the larger trees has a line of disturbed grass leading to it – could be animal, could be human. It's the acacia nearest you on a track of five to ten degrees from the pool."

"Hold a position down wind, at the maximum height for continued ground recognition. If there's anyone out there they'll think you've moved off.

You two, check out that acacia."

∞

Gillmor and Smit were halfway towards the tree when Smit's radio crackled.

"We have infrared back, looks like one under the

tree nearest to you, horizontal to the ground."

"Smit, get up the hill and come in from behind. If it's Legachev, sort him out. I'll walk straight at him as a distraction. He won't shoot somebody he doesn't know." Gillmor said.

After Theo talked with the chopper pilot he paced the length of the hallway to find the Boss-man.

"Sir, we have a security alert. It's low priority but probably better to delay your swim until we've checked it out."

"Seriously? Are we capable of being threatened here, in Constantia Nek?"

"I'm not certain, but fifteen minutes, that's all it'll take."

"Take for what?"

"To see whether Vitali Legachev is hiding in the long grass, pointing a weapon our way."

"Legachev? Guns for poisoned rain? He was pretty pissed about the whole affair. Okay, say when it's clear."

∞

Gillmor walked towards the acacia at a steady but slow pace, while Smit ran for his life under cover of the tall pearl millet grass, achieving the distance needed to come in unnoticed from behind.

Vitali patiently watched Gillmor's casual approach, with rivulets of adrenaline-induced sweat flowing through the fleshy ravines of his chiselled face.

Vitali was calm, and as the distance between them closed, he slowly covered the gun's trigger with a relaxed index finger. At fifteen metres he would have to shoot. Yet unaware that Gillmor knew of his presence he was suddenly surprised.

"Mr. Legachev."

While Gillmor waited for an answer he watched Smit silently positioning himself.

Vitali came to his feet, pointing his weapon directly at Gillmor.

"Who are you?"

"My name is Gillmor."

"What do you want?"

"I'd like to talk with you, about what you're doing

here."

Smit step forward without a sound, raise both hands behind Vitali's head and leant forward, encircling Vitali's neck with his steel garrotte.

"So far from home, and never to return." Smit said.

With the pleasure of pulling hard on the garrotte, Smit smiled, allowing the sun's reflection to sparkle from his silvered tooth.

Vitali dropped the rifle to wrestle briefly with the garrotte.

Smit gave both toggle ends a powerful last tug, and watched Vitali's writhing body slow to a twitch, before expiring.

A Sales Visit

Bagdad

The quartet that murdered Vitali Legachev were a highly efficient close-knit team of killers. At one time they were a quintet, but the emotional stress and moral impermissibility of their conduct forced Stefan Taylor to access an early exit and, well, as you know, he shot himself through the thigh to accelerate a discharge from the Recces.

The foursome had been operational in various arenas, sometimes killing individuals, such Vitali Legachev and Jose Branco, oft times killing hundreds, as they did in countless cross-border incursions into Angola, and sometimes killings thousands, which is why on one occasion they visited Iraq. Of course, they also assassinated Samora Machel, President of Mozambique, along with Andrew Mopeli's wife.

By rights they should all be standing trial at the International Criminal Court in the Hague, for crimes against humanity. Yet, as it happens, none of them make it to the end of this story, and that, believe me, is not a bad thing.

In Iraq, oil fields are everywhere, and along the country's southern border with Saudi Arabia herds of nodding donkeys are all the eye can see. Few icons of the fossil fuel industry are as familiar as the donkeys – unchanged in 100 years, pumpjacks is their original name. Here and there, as one donkey zone gives way to another, and in the un-pockmarked margins surviving between them, an irrigated date-farm will prosper, almost lugubriously, and in some of the highest summer temperatures in the world.

Yet atop the Euphrates Hotel in the centre of Baghdad, the morning that Theo Mason was there sucking at a large peach and squinting through the Tigris River's glare at the Bab al-Wastani below him, it was a comfortable twenty-five degrees. Theo wasn't alone, the other three were with him – Smit, drinking a mint tea, was quietly absorbed by the front-page story in the English edition of the Baghdad Observer, while Gillmor worked his way slowly through a thick date muesli. Plus, partially obscured by an outsized deep-green fig leaf, was their commanding officer – the Boss-man, a nickname from his position with the Bureau of State Security (BOSS). The Boss-man was sitting contentedly with a calculator and a note pad, deaf and blind to all but the silent pulse of electronic addition and the light emitting diode of its sum.

There was rank in this anarchic foursome, they were all serving, yet importantly, moonlighting, officers in the South African Defence Force. The Boss-man was a Lieutenant General, appointed personally by Jacko, but known only by his nickname, effectively remaining anonymous. Theo Mason was a Brigadier, and Johann Smit and Pik Gillmor were Majors.

"Seen this?"

Smit held the Baghdad Observer aloft for Theo and Gillmor.

"I recognise Saddam Hussein." Theo said.

"Who's the guy with him on the end of the sofa?" Gillmor said.

"A conservative minister from the UK, one of Thatcher's boys. Jesus, listen to this kak."

President Hussein asked that his greetings be conveyed to the British Prime Minister, together with Iraq's wish to develop friendship and co-operation with Britain on the basis of mutual respect and joint action to promote peace, security and stability.

"Mutual respect? What a fucking joke." Smit said.

"Theo, why is a British Minister in Bagdad, having his picture taken with Saddam on a dodgy looking chaise longue?" Gillmor said.

"The UK has a delegation camped out in Baghdad, and for the same reason we're here now, to arm and rearm Saddam."

The Boss-man pushed his calculator to one side and joined the conversation.

"The British are supplying millions of pounds' worth of machine tools, and a gun-cum-missile launcher, A super gun, something capable of thwacking anyone in the region but most probably the Kuwaitis. Reuben Shavit bribed the Iraqi procurement guys to get us in here, but before that the British had it all their own way for decades. Still, after our delivery to the Muthanna gasworks yesterday, Saddam needs a whole lot less hydrogen cyanide."

"Fucking hypocrites, the British. On the one hand they're down in Pretoria propping up the black elites, telling us we're white supremacists, and on the other they're here in Baghdad rearming Saddam."

"Theo, you're right. The British are scurrying around at the moment as guests of the Saddam, picking up gifts and mementos, and whatever else you might pick up in the backstreets of Baghdad.

I need to go, I'm off to sit on a dodgy chaise longue with our friend and benefactor. Okay, enjoy your afternoon, you deserve it. You know the score for the morning, reception, sixish."

"Yessir."

∞

Later in the day Smit and Gillmor hit street level, beered up, bought a pack of cigarettes and found a seat in the shade.

"Smit, this country's grotesque. We're restocking Muthanna gasworks with nerve gas as if we're bringing in medical supplies. And Saddam, he likes to despatch his enemies personally, with his ivory clad handgun, and the British praise him for maintaining security."

"I know, all you and I ever did was to protect ourselves from insurgent blacks intent on murdering us, and we were condemned by the whole fucking world. Crazy. We saved white lives, I don't have any qualms." Smit said.

"Yeah, that's as maybe, but we don't have any justification for what we're doing here. You know, Saddam's men torture and execute children in front of their parents. I can't go there, the idea I'd walk into a cell with the whole family present, and set about torturing the child to death, with the pain and violence and the fucking noise that would create. It's beyond me. You know, we're no ordinary soldiers, we're Recces, we're experienced combat commandos, but we would never do what these people do."

"Fuck." Smit said.

Somehow, Gillmor didn't think Smit wasn't using

the expletive in condemnation, he sensed the emotion for Smit was one of arousal.

∞

The following morning the foursome flew home to South Africa. Theo enjoyed the view of Baghdad disappearing beneath him, and Smit was absorbed with a fresh edition of the Baghdad Observer. The newspaper carried a front-page picture of the Boss-man, tricked by Saddam into bowing his head in respect. Saddam would hold his hand deliberately low and, in attempting to shake it, his guests were forced to look down – bow – rather than risk shaking some other part of Saddam's anatomy, and for that moment the host's photographer was always ready.

The Boss-man was considering the Iraqi offensive launched earlier that morning against the Kurds – he knew it would be a success, a short-lived zapping ending in thousands of deaths, men, women and children, asphyxiated by a cocktail of chemical and biological pathogens.

Getting To Know Your Brother

Bazaruto Mozambique

Jabu offered Gladstone a cigarette, which he took and lit, inducing a spluttering wheeze from his old lungs. After thanking him for the tour, Moses and Jabu walked back to their rondavel and lay on their money, and for more or less the whole of the following day, they lay on their money.

Wary of the potential for loss, Moses was incapable of being away from the stash. Yet the boredom was getting to him, and every hour or so he would start a session of press-ups to relieve the tedium. Jabu didn't register much of what was happening when Moses began, but then he counted over a fifty in a single session, and that rekindled his curiosity. Jabu could only ever remember his brother with muscles.

"Moses, how d'you get into this fitness stuff?"

Moses locked his arms straight on an up lift and answered.

"Jabu, when you were seven years old, I moved out. I was seventeen. I went to Ethiopia."

"You never did do that, Moses. What you lying to me for, you went to college."

"That's what Ma told you. I went to Ethiopia, Addis Ababa, got a training with a small bunch of ANC recruits, including the now-famous Andrew Mopeli and Frank and Georgie Mandoba."

"Moses, you no need to impress me, stop fucking lying. We both know who Andrew Mopeli is, and there's as much chance of you knowing him as there is of you becoming a church minister. And Cyril's never said anything 'bout Frank and Georgie being ANC."

Moses unlocked his arms and rolling to one side.

"Jabu, you asked the question, listen up a bit. Nine of us were smuggled out on the railroad to Bulawayo, and then to Addis Ababa. We met a guy from the Ethiopian military who took us to Kolfe, where the country's riot police were based."

"Man, this is too much."

"A year later I could shoot mortars, rifles, pistols, you name it. I learnt about conventional warfare, guerrilla warfare and germ warfare. On top of that I got fit, and I've kept it up. You never knew 'cos Ma decided it was better that way."

"What d'you do for the next two years, at college? You didn't come home."

"Got a job."

"What d'you work at Moses?"

"I was a freedom fighter, Jabu."

"You fucking me again?"

"No. I was based at a camp in Angola, running a training cell and at nights crossing the border into South Africa to blow things up."

"Fuck. Moses, d'you really know Andrew Mopeli?"

"Yeah, he's a good guy, and he's smart. I just can't get this amnesty thing he's pedalling, too many guilty people are gonna walk."

"Yeah, but it's the same for the ANC."

"The fuck it is. Jabu, we was a liberation army, we don't need forgiving."

"Exact same song the army's singing, 'cept they were freeing the country from ANC-inspired terrorists."

"Freeing the country? Jabu! The fuck they were, they ran a system that chewed up blacks and spat 'em out dead. Fucker."

"Moses, what you's saying, I know all that, don't get het up at me, but you ain't got a choice; you can't lock a whole population of whites up, throw away the key. These people need to tell what they did, the amnesty thing's okay."

"Jabu, we were justified, the armed resistance was a last resort, we talked to the bastards for half a century."

"That's where it fucks up when people start justifying. Moses, you can't justify murdering a farmer in his bed, just cos he's white, fuck what he's done. And Moses, you and your brothers in arms, you can't justify raping his children, ever. Justifying violence, people get it wrong. Whole societies get it wrong."

"You've got a lot to say." Moses said.

"All it takes, brother, is a few years of college. But there's a downside, I'm deficient in freedom-fighting skills. Moses, what happened to the Mandoba brothers?"

"Nobody knows. I went to Angola and Frank and Georgie returned to South Africa, began work with an ANC unit in Natal. Two years later Cyril got a photograph in the post, that's all he ever had, two of 'em shot in the head."

∞

It wasn't until Saturday morning that the brothers ventured out. They strolled off towards Ponta don Carlos on the north of the island, where according to Gladstone, they'd find a small shebeen come café.

En route they passed a huge tall sand dune. It resembled a gigantic wave about to break over them. Its concave face and arched crest had been shaped over time by the constant on shore wind at the headland, the same wind that spat sand and salt at the brothers. Although the café was unnamed an enamelled Coca-Cola sign hung over the entrance. It jarred against the vibrant orange paint of the roof's corrugated iron.

Moses and Jabu sat outside in the sunshine on rickety chairs. They drank a couple of cold beers, part way through another hard day in paradise. To their right was a small lagoon, its languid water being sieved through the bills of a hundred or so pink flamingos. And in the margins, around the lagoon's outflow, where the water was slightly brackish, a brood of white pelican chicks sat with their mother, bobbing on the surface, picking off occasional small fry swimming past in a dash towards the open sea.

"Where's ya man pelican?" Jabu said.

"Gone to the city to find work." Moses said.

"Jesus, yes. Down a gold mine?"

"Maybe he's on the way home." Moses said.

"Anyway, forget that, and talk to me about the money, where we gonna put it? Can't let it rule our lives, man, like yesterday – 'cos you insisted, we babysat a pile of serial numbers."

"I think we have to bury it," Moses said.

"It's already buried."

"I know, but that's not what I mean. We need a

hand-held GPS and some containers, watertight. We need to split the money, say a quarter million to each container. And then bury the containers at different locations, record the coordinates in the GPS, accurate to within thirty centimetres."

"Cool, and we won't have to wear an eye patch or draw a treasure map, but Moses, we's on an island in the Indian Ocean, off the coast of Mozam-fucking-bique. Where you gonna get a GPS?"

"The Cessna pilot who flew us to Vilanculos had one. Private pilots use 'em all the time, but they are not part of the aircraft, they're portable. I think we've got enough cash to do a deal."

"Isn't that like, asking for a wing, or a propeller?"

"No, they can navigate without GPS, it's an effort, that's all."

"Okay, that just leaves us to work out what'll happen next Thursday, when the real Roli and Milton pitch up."

"If they arrive, then we won't be here. If we're here, they won't arrive."

"You's doing riddles now?" Jabu said.

"We'll have bought them off, or not. Let's go to Vilanculos, see if we can find somebody to intercept them, and we can put some feelers out for a GPS, and a dentist. How's the varnish?"

Jabu exposed three broken but shiny teeth. "Okay, 's good."

They strolled back to their rondavel over trillions of crystal grains which ringed the Bazaruto shoreline with startling whiteness. Their barefoot imprints filled with seawater as the ocean lapped gently over the sea-polished quartz. They passed a couple chatting on sunbeds under a thatched parasol, large cocktails in hand. Moses responded to their friendly hello by nodding, oblivious to Stefan and Emma's conversation.

∞

Emma was sucking on her margarita.

"You're too hard on yourself," she said. "It's all very well in hindsight, saying it wasn't justified, but it didn't seem like that at the time, when you were responding to unprovoked aggression."

"That's what I believed in the beginning, but I didn't know the military was playing a double game with its own people. When we charged around Angola shredding the Cubans, we didn't know they'd been invited. Our military described them as unwelcome communists, expanding their sphere of influence in the world. The reality was totally different. Agostinho Neto's MPLA had asked Fidel Castro for combat troops, for protection, and to fight Jonas Savimbi, which seems a bit heavy-handed until you realise that Savimbi's UNITA party was virtually invented, funded and armed by the South African Government."

"You mean, we were the aggressors?" Emma said.

"Yeah, that's it – Neto's MPLA and the Cubans were acting in self-defence. We were the insurgents, and what we did was obscene, murdering people if we disagreed with their politics, or didn't like the colour of their skin, or if we thought they might disturb our way of life, our intrinsically wrong way of life."

"Stefan, that stuff at Kassinga, with Smit, that was obscene. I'm not surprised it haunts you. I still think the idea of talking to Andrew and the Ethics Committee is a good one."

"I need to get it out of me." Stefan said.

"How do you think Smit will react if you give evidence?"

"It's tricky, I wouldn't know without asking. I could talk to him, sound him out."

∞

Jabu left Moses to walk on home to the rondavel, while he walked on alone to the bar.

"Hi Naomi, how is it?" he asked, strolling towards her.

"Milton, the very person. Where's Roli?"

"Has this need to lie down."

"In case you're thinking of asking, I'll have a beer, and bring it over to the table, there, in the corner." Naomi said.

Jabu sat down opposite Naomi and pushed a beer forward, raising his own and smiling.

"Normally, when I bring the police from

Vilanculos, it takes about an hour – that's how long you've got." Naomi said.

"What you say? Got for what?"

"That's how long you've got, full stop. I got a letter this morning. It said, with regret, because of changed circumstances, that our offer of employment would no longer be acceptable. And who do you think it was from?"

"Somebody doesn't know how beautiful you are, or they'd be here." Jabu said.

"It was from Roli Khumalo, on behalf of himself and guess who, his brother, Milton. And if that was a hyena chewing your ear, then I'm a flea-infested, termite-eating aardvark. So what's the score, wise boy?"

There was no way for Jabu to know that Naomi was tracing the line of his lips, or that she was tingling with the thought of touching him.

"Shit. Naomi, we can't discuss this in the open. How about the office?" Jabu said.

He was playing for time, but Naomi, without a thought, which presumably made the lie compulsive, said the office was booked for a training session.

'Come to my rondavel." She said.

How Could Anyone Rhyme Root with Foot?

London

I slipped down through London's dark wintry sky shortly after six on Sunday morning, a good two hours before sunrise. Rosy watched me emerge into the international arrivals hall of Heathrow's terminal four. Outside a crusted white frost covered the ground, and there was a brittleness in the misty air.

"Christ, it's bloody freezing." I said.

"Northern hemisphere, polar bears, no penguins. Father Christmas, reindeer. Tim, it's winter."

"Okay, I got it."

"Good flight?"

"Just brilliant, thank you. I even had a massage."

∞

There was a gratifying clunk as Rosy operated her car's central locking, and a surprise for me when I saw the lights flash on a topaz-blue, ragtop Jaguar.

"Very nice."

I climbed in and gazed at the car's tech-savvy dashboard, totally unaware of Rosy's thinking, until that is she put a hand on my shoulder and leant forward to spread her lips over mine. She pulled back slowly, starring into my presumably dazed eyes. Rosy turned the ignition key and blew me a kiss, which I returned. I didn't know exactly what but something had changed, something had returned, something meaningful had embraced us both.

∞

Rosy closed her apartment door and leant back against it, waiting for me to register her stillness. When I did, she beckoned to me and, with one hand held in the nape of my neck, she kissed me again, deliberately and calmly. Afterwards we held hands and Rosy led us to her bedroom, to make love, and to confirm that meaningful change in our lives. The couple we had become, through years of involuntary disparateness, dissolved without trace, and the couple we would be emerged. We rekindled a familiar temerity, and an empathy that allowed us to promise each other all, forever, yet without saying a word.

∞

After breakfast we set off on foot to St Paul's Cathedral. Our breath turned to mist in the cold air, and our eyes told us both we were happy. From time to time there was a shaft of bright sunlight – the low winter beams zinged along the narrow city streets as we crossed between one high-rise block to the next.

"You were laying low in Gravelotte because this guy tried to kill you?"

"That's right."

"And an innocent woman died instead. That's shit! Tim, are you all right about what's happening?"

"I think so, but I need to get ahead of them, identify them, then I can fall back, take a view."

"We, we can take a view."

"Yes, mam."

∞

"What's special about St Paul's?"

Rosy asked the question with her neck craned upwards, looking at the cathedral's doom.

"Sir Christopher Wren is buried here, at the eastern end of the crypt. He was hauled up and down in a basket to inspect the work as it progressed, right up to the age of seventy-six. It's almost three hundred feet to the top, imagine his painstaking determination."

"Foolishness." Rosy said.

"No, determination. That's one reason I rate him, and his cathedral. It's the same type of resolve Tintoretto had, spending a lifetime painting the inside of a single house in Venice."

"The fresco cycle in the Scuola di San Rocco?" Rosy said.

"Yes, the fresco cycle. You might be a bit too bright for me."

"Might be!"

"Admiral Nelson's buried here as well, and Wellington, and John Donne, the poet."

"I know he's a poet."

"Pardon?"

"I know John Donne's a poet. You didn't say

Tintoretto the painter, or Admiral Nelson, the sailor, or the Duke of Wellington, the soldier. So, why say John Donne, the poet? Sounds like a piece of casual condescension to me."

"If you're that familiar with John Donne, let's have a few lines of his poetry then."

Rosy sucked her lips and thought for a moment, and to my astonishment began reciting a poem.

"Go and catch a falling star, get with child a mandrake root, tell me where all past years are, or who cleft the Devil's foot."

"Impressive! But perhaps Donne shouldn't be buried here after all, how could anyone rhyme root with foot? And what the hell's mandrake?"

"A good example of duality."

"Christ, did I start this?"

"Yep, you did. In small quantities mandrake is an aphrodisiac – get with child a mandrake root – but it's also a contraceptive.

"They used to say, Tim, being too much drank it drives out life. It expels the menstrua and ye embryo and being put up ye seat for a suppository it causeth sleep."

There was a short silence before we both laughed out loud.

∞

A while later we walked under the Tower of London's suspended portcullis.

"I've always been fascinated by the Crown Jewels." I said.

"Are you into cross dressing as well?" Rosy said.

"Rosy, should we ever get married, there is a possibility it might not work out. So, I was thinking, when we get to Tower Green in a moment, you might like to try out the beheading block for size."

Rosy pulled me towards her, smiling.

"In your dreams, boyo. What sensible girl would marry a hack working for a minority interest rag in the southern hemisphere?"

"Plenty, Andrea for starters." I said.

"Andrea? Andrea-with-the-lisp? Andrea besotted

with you at seventeen, Andrea?"

Even I was amused.

"Does she know you're psychotic, and that you harbour delusions of relevance for her?"

I leant forward and quietened Rosy with a kiss.

"Lunch?" I said.

"Please."

∞

At Giovanni's we spent time quietening and chatting. It was glorious. We followed a meandering conversation through the empty times and the back streets of our relationship, the years without nearness or touch, and we reminded each other of how things were shaped that way.

"I didn't want to go. Tim, I had no choice. South Africa stank. Staying meant colluding. I would have been complicit. Of course, I missed the country, the game parks, the reef snorkelling, the whale spotting, touching – you know, I've touched six whales. When we get back, I'll take you out on the water."

"You didn't want to go, and I didn't want to stay. It wrecked me when you left."

"It was fantastic when I first arrived in London. The whole world outside of South Africa was against apartheid, well, apart from a herd of political dinosaurs in the British establishment. The shout out was BDS – boycott, disinvest and sanction, and in the end it worked."

"You're right – in the end it worked, Mandela walked.

"Back then there were demos in Trafalgar Square every weekend, and I worked with the Free Mandela Campaign, it was a small thing but it made me feel connected."

"Back home I was reporting on the rise of Afrikaner fascism, a bunch of fat bastards on horseback. Rifles slung over their shoulders, bullet belts and grenades strapped to their bodies and swastikas on their arms."

"Lobotomised molluscs." Rosy said.

"Brilliant. Mind you, they marginalize us reporters by creating a censorial press."

"After the LSE, rather than being marginalized, I was assimilated. I bought a home in Chicago, a ticket for the local production of the American Dream and spent the next few years at The Chicago Commodity Exchange, first as a trader, making loads of money, and then as a director come techo, but using my specialist trader knowledge."

"And after Chicago, what did you do at Silverman's Bank?"

"Online security, yawn. The thing about online criminality is that the hackers are queuing to introduce themselves. It's an intellectual challenge for them, hacking a bank. There's a kind of old fashioned chivalry, good luck protecting your customers' money but let battle commence, and the hacker is somehow dishonoured if their presence goes undetected - they crave the attention, publicity, notoriety."

A Busy Day in Paradise

Bazaruto

For three days Smit moved north along the Mozambique coast, in pursuit of both Moses Kimbo and a cellular network for his mobile.

"I thought you'd have rung before now. How did you manage to fuck up a second time?" Theo said.

"You won't believe it."

"You're right."

"The Airbus made an emergency turn to avoid a bird strike, a fucking pelican, we were thrown all over the place. The syringe tip snapped off in a seat-back."

"Smit, the syringe tip didn't snap off in a seat-back, it snapped off in a Canadian lady's back."

"What?"

"You took out a Canadian business woman."

"Shit. I'll deal with Kitson as soon as I'm through here. Sir, I can't believe this is the right place. What led you to think Kimbo came here to Bazaruto?"

"I have a very reliable source in Maputo, he followed the bastard to Vilanculos, watched him catch a boat to the island. By the way, he's not alone."

"Who's with him?"

"Might be the guy gave you a bum steer in Jozi, apparently half his right ear's missing."

"That would make everything worthwhile, seeing him again. There's virtually nothing here, a couple of bars with cheap accommodation and an upmarket fishing lodge. If you're right they shouldn't be too difficult to find.

"Fuck. hang on."

Smit laid his phone on the café table, pulled the brim of his sunhat low and buried his face in a map of the island. He kept his head down for more than a minute, that's how long it took for a slow-walking couple to approach the café and pass by.

"Sir, Taylor's here. Stefan Taylor, with his new wife."

"Shit! Smit, take the initiative, approach them, say hello. Tell them you're on a week's holiday. Apologise for missing the wedding, I told them you had short-notice assignment."

"I'm not prepared for a holiday, I'll look a little odd on the beach, fully clothed, just a gun and a mobile. Get me some swimmers, Hawaii shirts, sunscreen, that sort of stuff. Give me a couple of hours, I'll text a drop coordinate, and keep the chopper on standby on the mainland, I'll need to get off here pretty quickly."

"Stay in touch, Smit."

∞

"Jabu, is that you?"

"Yeah, how's it going Moses?"

"I looked all over for you. It's ten in the morning."

"Moses, settle down."

Jabu entered the rondavel, dropped a bag by the door, lay down, plumped up his pillow and sighed in tiredness.

"Oh, Moses! I feel good, man. Okay, when we got back from the beach yesterday, you came to incubate ya money, and I went for a beer. Naomi asked for me to buy her one, and sit down, have a chat. Jesus, she frightened the shit out of me, said the mainland police were on the way to arrest us, cos we's impostors."

"How the hell did she work that out?"

"The Khumalo' brothers wrote Naomi a letter, said they'd changed their minds and weren't coming. Loud as you like, right there in the bar, she wants an explanation. I said to talk in her office but there was a training session, or something. Moses, man, she took me to her rondavel. Oh, Moses, talk 'bout clearing the brain, I never been laid like that before."

"You fucked Naomi? Jesus, what about the police?"

"Relax, it's sorted. And the truth is, Naomi fucked me, but she didn't fuck me, she made love, it was, oh, Moses."

"The plan was to keep a low profile."

"You'd have done the same. Anyways, we got talking; I told her about us and she was right into it, even offered to help."

"You told her?"

"She's given us a job in the kitchen, away from the public. And that bag over there, it's full of Tupperware containers, totally waterproof."

"You told her 'bout the money?"

"Naomi brings food from the mainland in them, they're airtight. Put the money in, run a tape round the top. It's okay, Moses."

"Fucker. Jabu, you fucker."

"It's cool, brother, and listen, there's a GPS, in the bag, belongs to the lodge owner, and he's away."

"You told her everything!"

"It was, ah, natural, man."

"Everything! That somebody shot your ear off. That we have $4m that's not ours buried in the ground here."

"Man, she's all right."

"Jesus, Jabu. Pass me a container, and the GPS."

"She's gonna keep her eyes open for anybody new or suspicious."

"This container stinks."

"Moses, it's probably the food. Christ, fishy – the label says essence of lobster."

While Moses unzipped the GPS and pushed its on-button, Jabu reached for more containers.

"Cheese," he said of the second, "and honey," of the third. "We can wash 'em in the salt water, easy. Oh, Naomi gave me a map." And he pulled it from his pocket to unfold on the ground between them.

"How many containers did you get?" Moses asked.

"You said a quarter of a million dollars each, that's seventeen. I brought sixteen, leaves a roll in our pocket."

"Okay Jabu, lots of four. Let's start in the north, around Ponta don Carlos, near the bar. Just here. We can use the sand dune and there's no tide in the lagoon, we can put them under water."

"Bury a couple in each location?"

"Yeah, and the dune's massive, so probably more later," Moses said.

By twelve thirty, a million dollars in four containers had been buried, and Moses and Jabu were clinking beer bottles in the sunshine. They'd gone a metre deep in the dune but reasonably shallow in the lagoon, where two metres of slack water covered its sandy bed.

At around five that afternoon, as they packed the last $1m, Naomi turned up to say hello at the rondavel.

Moses instinctively pushed the money behind him as she entered.

Naomi kissed Jabu on the forehead, sat between the brothers and spoke to Moses.

"You can trust me, it's okay." she said.

"Naomi, are your intentions with my young brother honourable?"

Moses beamed a wide smile, and after a moment so did Naomi.

"What's that smell?" She said.

"Lobster essence, mostly."

"Hey, you two, a new guest arrived, a Johann Smit. I don't think there's a problem because he's a friend of the honeymooners, but thing is, he fits the description you gave me, Jabu, of the guy who shot up your ear. He's really muscly, broad-shouldered, chunky, with short-cropped hair and blue eyes, but too close together, like you said."

"Jabu, you never described him like that to me. Naomi, was there anything else about him? Tell me about his face."

"Moses, you never met him."

"Jabu, listen up. Naomi, tell me about his face."

"It was ordinary, nothing special."

"What about his smile?" Moses said.

"I don't know. Umm, no, nothing special."

"Did he have a silver tooth?"

"Oh, yes he did."

"Shit, it is that thing. Moses, how'd you know he has a silver tooth?"

"At the bridge, he was there, pretended to be a policeman, said his name was Gary Roper."

"How the fuck did he find us here?" Jabu said.

"Naomi, where is he?" Moses said.

"Not sure, but he arranged to meet the honeymooners for sundowners, that's about now."

"Let's go see." Moses said.

Naomi led the way, through the back entrance of the lodge and around the dining room towards a door that opened onto an external food counter. She signalled for them to be silent and low, guiding them on her knees. The outside conversation was easily heard, and through a crack in the building's timberframe they were able to confirm

Smit's identity.

"I'm sorry, gate-crashing your honeymoon." Smit said.

"You weren't to know we'd be here." Stefan said.

"I heard your wedding was good fun."

"A really nice day, but the time flew." Emma said.

"There were a few celebrities, yeah? Dorothy Tutani, Andrew Mopeli, and that journalist, the political editor. What's his name?"

"Tim Kitson." Emma said.

"Yeah, that's him."

"He's a good friend of our family, used to be my sister Rosy's boyfriend years back."

"Smit, it's a strange coincidence, you pitching up here. Emma and I were talking about you only yesterday. There's an issue I'm trying to resolve, we thought it would be good to get your advice. You just mentioned Andrew Mopeli, I'm thinking of giving evidence to the Ethics Committee and applying for amnesty. What would you think about that?"

Smit couldn't say what he was thinking, which was *Stefan, you're fucking dead.*

"After you left the battalion, we came to a solid agreement that our names would never be released. I can't see how you would give evidence and allow us to retain anonymity. Your best man, Theo, he's a very close and old friend to you, but if you testify he will be forced to move against you, Stefan. I would move against you, neither of us through choice but because it's what would be expected of us, it would be our duty. Don't do it. Stefan, don't go anywhere near that Ethics Committee."

Naomi pointed silently at the return route and crawled away with Jabu following, but Moses stayed on to listen.

"It's easier for you, but Stefan still has nightmares about Kassinga, and about what the two of you did there." Emma said.

"I'll think on it, I owe you guys. Thanks for the drink, Smit. We're off to our chalet for a candle-lit dinner. Catch you later."

The Taylors headed off and Moses spent a few motionless seconds musing on what had been said, but as he turned to crawl away, Smit began a new conversation.

"Sir, we've got a problem. I haven't got to the Kimbos yet 'cos Stefan Taylor side-tracked me. The bastard wants to testify, apply for amnesty."

Silence.

"I know he's your friend, but giving evidence against us? When we discovered Jacko was going to do that he was dead within twenty-four hours."

Silence.

"There's nothing to think about, Sir. Give me the order."

"Fuck. Take him out." Theo said.

∞

Moses re-emerged into the dining room to find Naomi and Jabu kissing.

"Hey, we need to get out of here. Naomi, a couple of fishing boat radios, any chance? We can talk to you from the rondavel."

"Behind the reception counter, come over."

"Great. Naomi, wear an earpiece, I'll speak to you in a moment."

Moses gestured for Jabu to follow him and they moved together like bushmen, fast, almost unseen, through twilight to the rondavel.

"Jabu, there's a lot to do. Go bury the last four containers, and if I'm not here when you get back, just wait. Go.

"Naomi, can you hear me?" Moses said.

"I'm here."

"We're going to need a boat to get the honeymooners off Bazaruto. Can you arrange that?"

"No problem, but why?"

"No time, I'll tell you later. Naomi, I need Smit's telephone number. Check his registration card for contact details. If it's not there you'll need to get it some other way. I also need the last number he dialled, that won't be easy; you'll need to look at his phone."

"Hang on," she said. "Moses, he's just walking towards the loo, his phone's on the table."

"Go for it, be careful. Come over when you're ready.

If I'm not here, just wait.

∞

As Stefan opened his chalet door Moses pushed his forearm forward to shake hands.

"Good evening, sorry to disturb your candle-lit dinner." Moses said.

"How did you know?"

"Stefan, my name is Moses Kimbo. We have a mutual friend in Andrew Mopeli. We also have some mutual enemies, which is what I'd like to discuss with you. May I come in?"

"Emma, this is Moses Kimbo, a friend of Andrew's, he wants to talk with us."

"Stefan, you'll find what I have to say, shocking. Your friend, Theo Mason, he has just authorised your liquidation, your murder."

"Don't be silly, he's a good friend." Emma said.

"I'm not being silly, the conversation you had with Smit, about testifying, applying for amnesty, it wasn't well received. Theo ordered Smit to kill you, Stefan."

"Good God. How do you know that?" Emma said.

"Listen up, there's no time to explain. I've made a plan but you need to trust me. Ring Andrew and check me out. Say hello from me. I'll be back to collect you in thirty minutes. Be ready."

The Eve of The End of History

London

Rosy and I met Jim Trebor in the main lobby at Westminster – for me, two Parliaments in a week and a false sense of upward mobility. After a little helloing, Jim led us from the main building and along several back alleys to the Numero Uno Café in Gayfere Street, to a prebooked cosy, cubicle-table where we talked and drank coffee.

"Okay, if I understand correctly, going on what Toby Weinberg has told me, at the moment you're both living in Flatland." Jim said.

"Flatland?"

"Rosy, let me explain. Imagine a ball being thrown into water, but try to imagine it in two dimensions, which is not easy. In two dimensions the spherical ball is not visible. Instead, all you would see is a small hole appear on the water's surface, which would increase in size until it reached the ball's equator, it's widest part."

"Right." I said.

"Then, as the ball sank lower in the water, past its equator, the hole would begin to close over, decreasing in size until it disappeared. In two dimensions a sphere is not directly observable – all you can see is the effect of the sphere's progress."

"That's compelling." Rosy said.

"So, what haven't we seen?"

"I'll come to that in a moment, Tim. First, it's important to realise that the Russian harvest didn't fail because of an El Nino induced drought. The El Nino wasn't helping matters, but the reality is that the harvest was sabotaged. Well, not the whole harvest but enough to make the difference between needing to import grain or not. I know that for a fact, when I'm not being an elected member of parliament, I'm an agronomist. I was there, in Russia, advising on soil management, and I analysed the damaged wheat.

"A virulent defoliant was what wrecked the harvest. Mixed with sodium iodine, which by itself could have precipitated rain to ease the draught conditions, the defoliant went undetected. It was sprayed from the air with the approval of the old Russian apparatchiks – they thought it was a panacea to counteract the lack of rainfall. In fact, it was the sharp end of a covert operation run by your government, well, run by Jacko and his Recces on behalf of your government."

"Sodium iodine? Dorothy Tutani told me that Rainmaker used sodium iodine to alter the composition of clouds around Easthope, but apparently that also wrecked the crops." I said.

"You're right, and it's the same people. Rainmaker's testing was carried out in South Africa, both for the real product, to precipitate rain, and for the clandestine defoliant. The army worked through a corrupt Israeli arms dealer to sell it on, and he apparently negotiated with Russia to pay Jacko a small fortune on the side.

"How much is a small fortune?" I said.

"I don't know, $10m, $15m."

"More than that, I reckon it was $25m. Toby and I discussed a $25m bullion sale by the Russians, it took place around the same time. The sale proceeds were wired to an account in the British Virgin Islands, tracked to part of my country's military." Rosy said.

"It has to be the same deal. Tell us more Jim." I said.

"There was a string of front companies like Rainmaker, virtually an A to Z, Alpha Laboratories to Zambezi Trekkers – they were all run by Jacko and his boys, raking in a share from each of the illegal deals. A guy called Primakov brokered the Rainmaker defoliant deal on behalf of the Russians, and the middleman was an Israeli guy called Reuben Shavit – both were subsequently shot in the head by Vitali Legachev, a staunch communist who turned stones in odd places for years until he found the suppliers of what became known in Russia as the Poisoned Rain."

"What you're saying is amazing. It's difficult to

believe this started on our farm."

"Or that it had such far-reaching consequences. So, to appreciate the magnitude of what you didn't see, you need a feel for politics a couple of decades ago. Political institutions evolve over time, often through centuries of transition and social change, unlike the present South Africa, which was created in a flash of necessity, at the very moment the white dwarf of apartheid imploded.

"But how did apartheid disappear?"

Rosy and I were all ears.

"Go on." I said.

"There were no defining moments. I mean, during the French Revolution, palaces were stormed and delicate women beheaded in their petticoats. And through the ascent of English constitutional power, monarchs were executed and murdered, probably the most gruesome being Edward II at Berkeley Castle, a glowing poker inserted into his anus through a hollowed horn, the means of his demise and the complicity of his assailants anonymised."

"Yuk." Rosy said.

"Jesus Christ. You've a lot to answer for, you English." I said.

"Yes, truly. Anyway, during the 1980s there was a wholesale mutation of global politics. The colonialism that arose from the exploitation of world resources over a three-hundred-year period was all but spent, and bobbing in its wake were a trail of communal conflicts and bankrupt states across Africa and South America. According to Fukuyama, it was the eve of the end of history.

"In Moscow it became hard to get a meal, let alone a pair of Nike trainers, and nothing marks out political failure more starkly than the prospect of a people starving. The mayor of Moscow at the time was a plain-speaking and popular Boris Yeltsin, who had no difficulty putting the old-style cadres of the party under pressure for their agricultural ineptitude, which opened the door to younger men such as Mikhail Gorbachev, who patiently waited on the side lines for his opportunity to step forward.

"The country's top brass gathered south of Moscow on the prairies, inspecting the wheat fields and grappling with the prospect of a grain shortage on a scale never imagined. That's when action was taken – Primakov travelled to Tel Aviv in search of Shavit, and an exchange programme was put together providing Russia with an agricultural advisory team from Europe, of which I was a member. So, sitting comfortably?"

"Go." Rosy said.

"Jacko's superior, the Boss-man, to this day still anonymous, he single-handedly brought about the abolition of apartheid."

"You are joking me." I said.

"Jim, do you enjoy conspiracy movies?" Rosy said.

"I know what you mean, both of you. What you mean is that what I've just said sounds stupid. I agree with you, it does, but it really happened, and it doesn't end there."

"Doesn't end there?" Rosy said.

"The same person, he also brought about the dissolution of the Union of Soviet Socialist Republics."

"Brought down the USSR?" I said.

"Yes, the Boss-man's actions precipitated Glasnost and Perestroika which reformed the economic and political system.

"Jim, roll it out, please. It's too compressed for me." I said

"OK – first of all, the South African intention of sabotaging the harvest was to weaken the Russian economy, in the hope it could no longer afford to finance Angola and Mozambique in their border wars with South Africa."

"Interesting." Rosy said.

"Well, the defoliant deployment was spot on, fucked everything in its path. More than that, we discovered in the Moscow lab that it had a residual soil-based potency of five years – overnight the need for imported grain was beyond the country's means. Just months later, when Gorbachev was sworn in, what did we hear him say?"

"Glasnost, Perestroika, comrades - democracy, a market economy, the end of communism, the end of the USSR!"

"This is fucking amazing." Rosy said.

"By that year end Gorbachev was sipping cocktails

with Ronald Reagan at Camp David, and appearing in photoshoots with an arm around Margaret Thatcher. Gorbachev was networking, attempting to make economic friends in the West, needing to get the rouble integrated into foreign exchange markets. The Russian economy had been brought to its knees, importing huge quantities of grain and paying for it not with roubles but with gold."

"And the abolition of apartheid, Jim?" I said.

"Well, it's complicated but hang in there – so, at the same time Russia caused a reduction in the value of gold, by selling shed loads of it to pay for grain, the US Treasury dumped tons of it themselves, driving the price even lower. That action was part of a strategy to permanently devalue gold, forcing the use of the dollar as an international benchmark value – if the dollar offered a more stable value than gold, people would start trading in dollars, a huge advantage to the Americans."

"Jim, I get it, and Tim, the abolition of apartheid, I can see that – it was the gold price collapse. South Africa had a gold-based economy, overnight it was no longer viable, no longer capable of financing racism. Out of nowhere the country needed an educated and skilled workforce to modernise the country's economy."

"Completely right, Rosy, you have it. It's so ironic though, the Boss-man's original intention was to weaken international support for Angola and Mozambique and strengthen white supremacy at home." Jim said.

"Yet instead, he gave us our first black Government." Rosy said.

"The way he participated in his own liquidation is truly stunning. There are probably days when he'd welcome a bullet in the head." I said.

"OK, you two have left Flatland. A last thought, there are some powerful Russians who want their old USSR back – for them the Baltic States, Crimea, Ukraine and all their other lost homelands are still unconditionally Russian.

"I'm going to let you two pick up the tab. I need to dash. Great to say hello, feel free to ring, anytime."

∞

With that Jim Trebor was away, returning Rosy and I to our three-dimensional world – orbited, as if to prove the point, by a telecoms satellite in search of me.

"Hi," I said.

I answered the Post's satellite phone in tandem with an enormous clang.

"Christ, what's that noise? Sounds like..."

Clang.

"you're sitting alongside Big Ben in London."

"I..."

Clang.

"am," I said.

I was totally freaked and thinking fast.

"It's a screensaver-cum-alarm clock on the laptop, you even get..."

Clang.

"the city sound effects."

"From this end it's incredibly..."

Clang.

"realistic. You must show me when you get back."

Clang.

"How is it down in the bush?"

Clang.

"Pretty good, right place to have come." I said.

"And the story?"

"It's coming together, but slowly, it's complex. I'll email a piece for tomorrow but give me another forty-eight hours to produce something major."

"You need to hurry up, at the moment it's still a scoop. Why has Big Ben stopped at eight, it's ten?"

"It's British wintertime."

"Clever," Bruce said.

∞

"What was that about?" Rosy said.

"Bruce."

"Oh, and he didn't realise?"

"No."

"Brilliant."

"Fucking hilarious." I said.

"Next stop Washington?"

"Rosy, can you handle that? I need to write a piece for Bruce, and I'd like to get back and check a few things out. You go to Washington, have a great time, and then take a fast plane home to me."

"De novo," Rosy said, placing her hand on mine.

"What's that mean?"

"From the beginning. Anew."

The Boss-man

Washington

Rosy and I headed back to the Barbican to enjoy some old-fashioned horizontal refreshment. A few hours later we were accelerating apart at a thousand miles an hour, as I flew south over Africa and Rosy chased the sun through an un-darkening sky to Washington.

Toby Weinberg drove from his home in Rock Creek Park to collect Rosy the following morning, using a route that took him past the White House and the Lincoln Memorial, across the Potomac River and south past the Pentagon and the Tomb of the Unknowns. His return journey deviated at the Lincoln Memorial as he turned right off 23rd Street and drove along Constitutional Avenue. A mile and a half later he parked up in an underground lot adjacent to the National Archives and Records Administration.

"That was better than a guided tour; the only thing I didn't see was the White House," Rosy said.

The elevator sped to the thirty-eighth floor.

"I'll take you there later, most people are surprised by its smallness, but then it was designed by a child."

"What?"

"A French architect designed the original, a Pierre L'Enfant."

"Very funny, not."

"Fair enough." Toby said.

"Thanks for collecting me from the airport. So, what are we up to this morning?"

"The people I work with lifted surveillance and put a hold on this case a while back, but they didn't close the file. They'd still like to know how it panned out and who was involved. So, we grant you access to our database, and in return, when it's appropriate, you give us an update, fill us in on the details. Easy."

After several corridors and a few good mornings and hellos, Toby opened the door to a semi-darkened room, wallpapered with computers and flat screens.

"Morning, Daryl, Rosy Lennox. Rosy, Daryl Kerry."

Toby said.

"I've briefed Daryl on what you need, and I've explained the generosity of your offer to help us with this investigation."

At which point, apparently, Toby found the space to wink at Rosy without Daryl noticing, allowing her to appreciate the joke of what he was saying.

"Rosy, give me a ring when you're through. I'll leave you to it, and see you later. Daryl, start with the bank account."

"Rosy, have a seat. The British Virgin Islands' account is held with Fabio & Nicholson, a small merchant bank with offices in Italy and London. The account was opened in the name of Rainmaker, an organisation sponsored by the South African government, set up to destabilise the old USSR's economy, and incredibly it worked."

"Yeah, I've heard that, it's amazing."

"So, the Russians wired Rainmaker $25m. At that point the name of the account was changed to Project Costa, and various amounts were paid in to that account over the next few years, from all over the place, South Africa, Libya, Iraq, and even the UK. During that time we realised that Project Costa was selling chemical and biological weapons.

"So, you can see the screen ok, yeah? Rosy, we have a huge database and a stack of intelligence – you know, illicit arms deals, offshore accounts, dodgy politicians, corrupt officials. How can I help?"

"Thanks, Daryl. So, this whole thing began when a friend received a report in the post detailing the activities of Project Costa, but there were no names. We want to know who was involved, who is involved, what happened and what's happening now."

"Fine, here we go."

Daryl double-clicked through the projectcosta directory and stuck a finger on the screen.

"At the top was a General Jackson, better known as Jacko. The General delegated responsibility for Project Costa to an individual we have never positively identified – he's simply known to as the Boss-man. Below him was a Theo Mason, and the important players under his control were a small bunch of brain-dead stooges, including Johann Smit, Jon Gillmor and a Larry Lauderdale."

Rosy watched Daryl's finger move over the names in disbelief, unaware of the ashen hue that had bleached her complexion.

"Oh my God." She said.

"What?"

"I know these people. Fucking hell, Theo Mason was the best man at my sister's wedding."

Daryl repositioned the cursor, clicked through the relevant directories and zoomed in from outer space to Easthope.

"You probably know this place too."

"Shit. Daryl, why do you have a satellite image of my parent's home?"

"For a couple of years it was Rainmaker's home."

"Of course, yes, the guava orchard alongside the airstrip."

"We thought your father might be involved, but he wasn't, he simply rented the land. After Rainmaker moved out, a guy called Marty Schwartz took over the hangers, but he checks out too. He's often been hired as an air taxi or courier by Rainmaker but it was part of his legitimate business."

"The detail on these images is amazing. My God, that's Stefan, he's Emma's new husband."

"You don't need to worry about him. Stefan Taylor was instrumental in the set up phase but only as a regular soldier, well a reconnaissance commando, but he never went to Baghdad and back in South Africa he was never involved with the drugs trade."

"What happened in Baghdad?"

"The worst thing. The bastards delivery chemical and biological weapons to Saddam Hussein, and he used them."

"Jesus."

Rosy, have a browse through these jpegs while I get a coffee. What can I get you?"

"Tea, thanks. No milk. A green tea if you can find one."

Rosy began maximising the thumbnails. There was nothing familiar until the twentieth image, the start of a series from the Baghdad Observer, mostly of Saddam greeting foreign visitors. The one that caught Rosy's eye was a side on shot showing a clear profile of the visitor's face, his head was bowed and he was shaking Saddam's hand.

"I found some green tea with vanilla, any good?" Daryl said.

Before answering Rosy maximised the image and took a closer look.

"Fuck."

"You don't like vanilla?"

"No, that's great,"

"What have you found?"

"I've found the Boss-man." She said.

"Seriously?"

"The guy with his head bowed, shaking hands with Saddam. I recognise him, but you haven't mentioned him. If you don't know him, or his name, he's almost certainly the Boss-man."

"Who the hell is he?"

"Jordan Atwell. He was also at my sister's wedding. You know, it makes sense, nobody has ever understood how he made his money, and he's extraordinarily wealthy."

"Amazing. Rosy, this guy here by the way, Smit, he doesn't always use the same name. He sometimes masquerades as Gary Roper."

Christ Almighty. Every next thing. Gary Roper tried to kill Tim.

"How's your tea, Rosy?"

"Very nice. Thanks."

An Organic Bomb, Nancy's Murderer & Free Beers

Bazaruto

Moses ducked and entered the rondavel to find Naomi there alone, cross-legged in a flickering light, studying a map.

"Jabu not back?"

"Not yet, but the boat's organised. Gladstone's waiting with it on the beach. Moses, the next island out, Mazaleto, it's a better idea than the mainland. The island is secluded, and our tourist shack there is comfortable. Gladstone has a key and some supplies."

"Thanks Naomi. Did you get the number?"

"Yeah, in fact, two. Smit's number from the registration card, plus the last number dialled from his phone."

"Great, I'll ring them both tomorrow, should be fun. Okay, I'll go now and take the honeymooners to Mazaleto, back in an hour or so."

∞

"Jabu, is that you?"

"Yeah, how you doing, Naomi?"

"Good."

Jabu crossed the threshold and stepped fully inside the small interior.

"Christ! Jabu, you stink."

"I know, sorry. Essence of lobster, mixed with honey. I was in a hurry, washed the containers in the lagoon, don't clean like the salt water. And I left the tape behind, so they's only sealed with the lip of the container lids. I'll get back to them. Where's Moses?"

"Taking the Taylors to Mazaleto, back in an hour or so."

"That's long enough,"

Dropping to his knees, Jabu achieved a controlled flop.

"Oh, talk 'bout clearing the brain, Naomi, last

night, wow."

Watching Naomi fold under his weight, Jabu fell beside her, and Naomi pulled his full lips towards her.

∞

"It's not far, a mile, due south," Moses said.

Stefan stepped in alongside Emma and Gladstone gave the boat a push, while Moses encouraged a gentle purr from the boats small outboard.

"Stefan, what's happening? What do you know, makes them want to take you out?" Moses said.

"I was a Recce. We killed thousands of people. An assault at Kassinga and an operation code-named Stealth were really bad, solid shit. I've decided to go public, talk with the Ethics Committee, but others feel differently. Some are openly hostile, totally freaked about being identified for what they did."

"You were at Kassinga?"

"Yes, how do you know about Kassinga?"

"I read about it, and I can understand what you mean, about it being bad."

Stefan listened to the swishing water of their progress, and to the spluttering purr of the outboard, considered things.

"Moses, you didn't read about it."

"I didn't?"

"No, it's deliberately never been written about."

"No."

"So?"

"You remember Robert Dorado, the Liberation Army commander who escaped from Kassinga?"

After his question Moses rocked the boat a little, correcting its course in the darkness.

"Moses, who the fuck are you?"

"I am one of the very few people, along with Robert Dorado, who you didn't kill that day."

"Jesus!"

"Stefan, I wouldn't have said this a week ago, but Jabu has been chewing my ear."

"That's pretty ironic, given the way his looks right now."

"Yeah, anyway, Jabu has made me think I should

do it also, go public."

"That's a great idea. If the process was less one-sided it would mean that much more. If you and your blacks brothers start giving evidence alongside us, so much the better."

Moses dropped them ashore and headed off.

"Enjoy yourselves." He said.

∞

By seven thirty the next morning the Kimbo brothers were out and about, drinking coffee and listening to the rakishness of the waves at the nameless café.

"Make that call, man. Come on." Jabu Said.

"Calm down."

"Moses, there's an animalised humanoid creature wandering this island, this small island. It's the sort of creature bred to kill blacks, and Moses, it's looking for me. I can't calm down. Make the call, man."

After a little thought, Moses nodded, but then he was distracted. A shadow moved across their café table, darkening the dappled light from the fine-meshed cloth of the table's parasol. Then, without warning, there was a huge explosion and a hail of organic ammo – Moses escaped unscathed but Jabu was riddled, strafed from head to foot by pellets formed like shot in a tower, when molten lead is forced at speed through tiny holes.

Jabu looked up and screamed.

An enormous white pelican had emptied its bowels above their table, and the remains of two or three defecated fish had accelerated downwards, turning to shot as they sped through the tiny holes of the parasol's meshed cloth above Jabu's head.

"Jesus Christ! Jabu, oh, that's truly disgusting, what a fucking stench."

Moses was still speaking when he stood up and reflexively backed away from the table.

Jabu was a dripping and gasping mess. Small streams of excrement were trickling over his top lip and into his mouth, causing him to spit and scream a second time. Jabu jumped up and ran for the sea – pulling off his T-shirt and throwing it to the ground, shaking his head hard as he dived into the breaking waves.

Billy was unaware of his organic bomb's

devastation, and while Jabu squirmed with its wretchedness in the salt water, my life saving pelican friend crossed the lagoon majestically, skimming the heads of a hundred or so flamingos before landing feet-first with a deep croak, at the end of an eleven hundred mile journey – Cape Town to Bazaruto.

∞

As Jabu surfaced he saw Moses on his knees, squawking loudly and totally overcome with the violent emotion of convulsive laughter.

"You bastard, Moses, you laughing at me is not good."

Moses could hardly talk, but he managed to shout persuasively at Jabu.

"Go get changed. I'll meet you back here in half an hour. While you're gone I'll call the creature."

∞

"Hello."

"Good morning, is that Smit?" Moses said.

"Speaking."

"Tell me, are you feeling warm or cold this morning?"

"What are you talking about? Who is this?"

"Warm or cold in the context of hide and seek. Do you feel close or far away, from what you're seeking?"

"Who the fuck is this?"

"It's Moses Kimbo, and as you're not answering the question, allow me – you're cold, ab-so-lute zero fucking cold."

"How did you get my number?"

"Same way I got to know you intend to kill Stefan and Emma Taylor, but Smit, in less than an hour they'll touch down in Madagascar, and me and Jabu, we're in Malawi. That should piss Theo off, don't you think – the fact you've fucked up again? Not such a good week for you, Smit – Tim Kitson is still alive, the Taylors have slipped through your fingers, and you can't lay your hands on a Kimbo, let alone the money."

"Think you're smart, do you?"

"Not particularly, just amazingly rich."

"I've already laid my hands on a Kimbo, a pretty little thing she was too, and after I fucked her I shot her in the head. Her name was Nancy, ring any bells?"

Smit waited for a response, but he heard nothing. Moses had flicked his call on hold and shouted Nancy's name as loud as he could in a release of emotion. Moses wanted to hurl the phone at the nameless café's hard mud wall but he didn't, and a moment later with Smit none the wiser, he rejoined the conversation.

"I've never heard of her. Smit, have a nice time on Bazaruto, on your own."

It was a full two hours before Moses had enough composure to make a second call.

"Theo Mason?" Moses said.

"Who is this? You're on a dedicated number but I don't recognise your voice."

"No, we've never spoken, but you'll recognise my name. I'm Moses Kimbo."

"Don't fuck with me, Kimbo."

"You've been fucking with us for years, Theo."

"What do you want?"

"Value for money."

"What the fuck does that mean?"

"Smit – you sent him to kill us, but Stefan convinced him to let us live, in exchange for $4m. Ironic isn't it, Jacko and his friends paying for the Kimbo brothers' safe passage, and chucking in a little spending money. Smit will tell you we escaped, the Taylors to Madagascar and the Kimbos to Malawi – but you know the truth, we didn't escape. Smit murdered my cousin Nancy – I'd be happy for you to fuck him, that's what I'd call value for money."

∞

It was another paradisical day, the air's ambient warmth was reassuring, and the Indian Ocean's twinkling turquoise water helped focus the planet's beauty. Moses, having collected Stefan and Emma, was skimming the waves, heading the water-taxi back to Bazaruto.

"Mazaleto, it's amazing!" Emma said.

"Maybe Smit should have stayed on a bit. You could have enjoyed more time on the island." Moses said.

"Smit's a bastard," Stefan said, "a psycho, and he's not that bright. The others have pulled the wool over his eyes for years. Smit has helped them make a fortune but he won't see a penny of it. He hasn't a clue."

"Listen, Smit helped make up my mind about giving evidence.' Moses said.

"If you're up for it you can fly back with me. We've arranged for Emma to spend a few days in the bush, and I'm about to ring Andrew and let him know I'm coming – or is it we, Moses?"

"We. People like Smit carry on as if nothing has changed."

"Great."

"Moses, people like you, you'll make the difference."

∞

Jabu spotted Moses jogging around the beachhead point towards Naomi and himself.

"I'll get him a beer." He said.

Jabu reappeared and they watched Moses arrive, with Naomi feeling lucky to have met the Kimbos.

"I used the phone again, owe you for two calls." Moses said.

"Who'd you call, brother?"

"I had a second word with Smit, to let him know his superiors are ripping him off, thought it might spark him up a bit. I also rang Tim Kitson to let him know who I am and to pass on a few names that Stefan gave me.

"Moses, would you like fish puree for lunch?" Naomi said.

Moses spluttered into his beer.

"What's it like?" He said.

"Ask Jabu, he had it yesterday."

"Would you recommend it, Jabu?"

"Fuck off, the pair of you."

"Oh my God. Pelican alert." Moses said.

"Quit fooling about." Jabu said.

"Jabu, turn around." Moses said.

"Shit, there's something in its mouth, maybe a fish. He's heading straight for me. Why me?"

Jabu's screaming was enough to attract Franklin Tabayama's attention, and bring the bar's owner out to have a look at what was happening.

"If it does it again, you clean up today." Franklin

said.

"Jesus, what's in his mouth? It's too big for a fish." Jabu said.

"Shit, it's really wobbly. Run for it." Moses said.

Franklin stood his ground, mesmerised by the pelican's offering, which fell from its mouth and sped downwards, splat into Franklin's chest. The impact triggered a catch but before Franklin's right hand could move to stem the flow the aerial gift burst open and thousands of dollars rose into the air. There was a pervasive smell of lobster essence, and a stunned silence from everybody but Franklin.

"It's free beers all day. All week." He said

Franklin was smiling at the smelly fortune in his hands.

∞

Later, while the sun set in a white-and-orange blaze, and with Moses gently shaking his head, he turned to Jabu and eyed him sternly.

"FREE beer! FREE!" He said.

"We's had five each, that's a total of ten," Jabu said.

"Great, just $25,000 a beer then."

"Well, if we's have another ten it'll halve the price."

"And if, Jabu, by the end of the week we've drunk a hundred and twenty-five thousand beers each, we'll have got them at the going rate. Even then, they won't be FREE!"

"I'm sorry, but I buried the last couple of containers in a hurry, you know that, and anyways Moses, we's still got a fortune."

"And what other enticing flavours have you buried?"

"Honey, but just one container, I washed the rest in sea water."

"And does the island have a swarm of intelligent bees?"

"Fuck knows. Moses, stop it. Tell me what's happening."

"Stefan's arranged to see Andrew on Friday, I'm going with him. We'll leave tomorrow. Emma's travelling back via Gravelotte – Tim Kitson offered her his bush hut there to lie low – reckons until Smit's taken out of circulation it's safer. And Jabu, you can stay here, carry on clearing the brain."

"OK brother. Let's go get another FREE beer."

Count Von Caprivi & His Ruler

Jozi

I collected Rosy from her Washington flight and drove us home to my Jozi apartment. Once there I steamed some milk for a couple of cappuccinos and carried them to my kitchen's breakfast bar, where I sat, in anticipation.

"Lots to tell me?"

"Bet your life, boyo. Would you like to know the Boss-man's identity."

"No! How did you do that?"

"I recognised a photograph of him in the Baghdad Observer."

"Sorry? The Baghdad Observer?"

"Yeah."

"Where did you see a copy of that, and who the hell is he?"

"Jordan Atwell."

"Atwell. Fuck me. He's always been a suspicious sort."

"Guess who's with Atwell in the Baghdad Observer, and I'll give you a clue. Like you, he thinks the pen is mightier than the sword."

"Andrew said that about me at the wedding."

"It's not him though."

"What are you talking about?"

"Ah, this guy murders women on aeroplanes."

It took a few seconds – the ornate pen, Rosemary Windsor, Billy saving my life.

"Roper? Gary Roper?"

"Yeah, but that's an alias, his real name is Smit, Johann Smit."

"Fuck!"

"What?"

"I had a call from a Moses Kimbo – turns out he's the guy who mailed me the reports – and this is weird, he said he just helped save Stefan and Emma's lives, foiled a murder attempt by a guy named?"

"Smit?" Rosy said.

"Yeah."

"Tim, are they okay?"

"Don't worry, they're fine. But Rosy, Kimbo said Smit was acting on Theo Mason's orders, so if Mason told Smit to kill Stefan and Emma, he presumably told Smit to kill me."

"The fucker. We're talking about the best man at my sister's wedding."

"I know. It's unbelievable."

"Fucker."

"Rosy, at Westminster, Zambezi Trekkers was mentioned as a front company. It took me by surprise because years back Atwell was rumoured to be involved with that company – they did a lot of sanctions busting on the upper Zambezi around the Caprivi Strip."

"*Around* a Strip?"

"Yeah. Count von Caprivi, arrogant Eurocentric. Caprivi created the strip in the eighteen hundreds, with his ruler. He joined together the remote scrubland of five countries and unintentionally created a smugglers' paradise. It happened at the Berlin Conference, all part of the scramble for Africa. Years later an Imperial Airway's captain landed his flying boat at the eastern end of the strip, on his way from London to Jozi. Bobbing in the river, surrounded by tropical plants and screeching monkeys, he named the stopover Jungle Junction. But the cartographers in London took the captain not so much at his word as at his circle drawn on the chart. The J of Jungle was in Botswana and the J of Junction in Zambia – which is how Jungle Junction became a place and an area, *around* the Caprivi Strip.

"Anyway, Atwell must have realised I could link him directly to Project Costa, via Zambezi Trekkers if they were listed in the report. He even rang to tease out of me which companies were named. I didn't tell him but I suppose he thought it best to assume the worst."

"And blow us both to fuck."

"Yeah. Rosy, this guy Moses, he knows Andrew. I rang to check him out and they go back years. Also, apparently, Moses and Stefan are giving evidence to

Andrew in the Ethics Committee."

"That is so good – Emma's been pushing Stefan that way."

"Hey, tell me about Washington."

"Nice cappuccino, thanks. Right. Jacko was at the top. He delegated Project Costa to Atwell. Below Atwell was Theo-Fucker, and the important players below him included Smit, Jon Gillmor and Larry Lauderdale.

"For a short while Stefan was involved, but legitimately and only at the beginning. Daryl said he left the army early on before criminality became a way of life.

"Something else, the fortune they amassed, it's stashed in the British Virgin Islands and we have the bank account details. Daryl reckons Atwell is controlling the whole thing with a laptop and a satellite phone."

"How does that help us?"

"It doesn't. It helps me. You're after the baddies, remember, 'cos that's what you do, being an investigative journalist. Me, being a banker, I'm after the money, and at the risk of annoying you I've asked Peter Lipscombe to help me find it."

∞

Later that morning I took a seat to the right of Bruce Pontin in the daily news conference – the intention being to speak last after having gauged the mood. Yet when Bruce brought us to order I was surprised.

"Normally, we run clockwise, this morning I'm reversing the order. Tim, we'd all like to know why you intend to write a banal piece of drivel for this evening's edition, rather than the scoop of the year that you've been promising. We would also like to know whether the addled nature of your thinking is in anyway attributable to the phenomenon of spaced-out-ness often engendered in male by the prospect of love."

"Very fucking funny. I am not addled, and I am not spaced out."

"But you are in love?" Bruce said.

"It's none of your business."

"Right, back to the banal drivel." Bruce said.

"I don't write drivel. I know the pieces so far haven't said a lot, but that's been intentional. This is the deal, by not going public now, within days we'll have a scoop twenty times as big, and it'll be an international story. The Government wants Project Costa's Boss-man behind bars. He is presently running the largest drug manufacturing operation in the southern hemisphere and even those in the Government who support the Ethics Committee's work don't want this man to walk. I've had two meetings with Joshua Chios of the Justice Department and, fully sanctioned from above, he has offered me fly-on-the-wall access to whatever unfolds, as long as we play along with them for the next forty eight hours. The two-year period for the admission of evidence ends tomorrow, and with it the opportunity of amnesty."

"Tim, sorry to interrupt, do we know this guy's name?" Bruce said.

"Yes, but that's exactly what we want to convince him we don't know, his name, his identity. If we can do that he won't put his hands up and surrender, but if he feels we can nail him, there's every chance he'll play safe and confess."

"What you're suggesting raises some ethical issues of our own, printing lies, deceiving the public. Apart from that, is this why Joshua Chios resigned from the Ethics Committee last week, because he wants the man nailed and Andrew Mopeli wants him forgiven?"

"More or less. Somebody else you should think about is me – they've already tried to kill me twice. It'll take the heat off, running the story I'm suggesting, which probably means, you'll be pleased to hear, I'll be around a little longer for you to ridicule."

"That's a good enough reason for me." Bruce said.

∞

Rosy settled herself into the extravagance of a deep leather sofa, and admired the art on the walls.

"You're doing very well, Peter."

"They made me Chairman."

"It's great of you to fit me in, thanks."

"No problem. Rosy, I'm just sorry I only have this short slot, lunch would have been so much nicer. There are some sandwiches on the way."

"No, this is perfect."

"Okay, what can I do for you?"

"The fact that you're a friend is an important part

of why I'm here. I need someone who can trust me. I want to talk to you about a very delicate issue, and if I discussed it with any other banker in the city they'd have me arrested before I left the building."

"And I won't, because I trust you? Oh shit."

"I need an assurance. Confidentiality. Can you give me that?"

"Difficult, without knowing what you're going to tell me, but I will, I suppose. I mean, Rosy, we are friends, aren't we?"

"Okay, I'm currently working with the CIA."

Rosy, knowing full well she wasn't working for the CIA, had learnt enough from Toby Weinberg to say as much without feeling awkward or disingenuous.

"Good God." Peter said.

"I'm helping them investigate a prominent South African who has amassed a fortune from the proceeds of crime. Although his arrest is in the interests of our own Government, they are currently unaware of what's happening. It needs to stay that way for the moment. If they find out what's going on they'll rush in and blow the whole operation, and any chance of recovering the money from this guy will be lost. Hence the delicate nature of what I'm telling you."

"Okay, so what can I do?"

"Karl Jones, who used to work for me in London, is still head of your IT division. I'd like to pick his brains."

"I remember when he applied here, you gave him a glowing reference. That's easy enough. Tomorrow?"

"If he's free I could be here for eleven."

"I'll make sure he's free."

"Great, give Karl my number and I'll brief him before we meet. Moving on, Peter, what's the current discretionary limit on automated transfers from overseas?"

"Lipscombes is delimited, but we do have a report threshold. Deposits of $500m and over require reporting. We're obliged to submit sender and recipient details to the Treasury."

"And how is it made operational? Per client, per account?"

"It's notifiable on a monthly cumulative figure. Notifiable is the official word, although in my vocabulary the word only applies to infectious diseases, rabies, foot and mouth."

"Perhaps some overseas deposits are infectious."

"Maybe, well, cartel money is nasty stuff."

"So, cumulative, and then?"

"Per client, and basically that creates a reasonable level of transparency."

"Okay. So, I'd like to open an account."

"A new customer, at least there's something in this for me. Personal? Business?"

"Ah no, it's a charity account. I've asked my solicitor to send you the paperwork, stated aims, registration certificate, usual stuff."

"Fine, if I get you to sign some bits and pieces now I'll open the account when I receive the documentation. What's the charity called?"

"Amakhaya."

"That's Xhosa for homes, yeah?"

"Yeah, but it's the same word in Zulu, so easy recognition. Peter, would you also open an account in the British Virgin Islands with Fabio & Nicholson, and another in Switzerland, any bank will do there."

"Fabio & Nicholson! Christ, the money they handle is filthy even though it gets laundered on a daily basis."

"What do you know about them?"

"Not a lot, apart from their reputation, which is pretty grubby. It's more my old man's era than mine. There was always a rumour in banking circles of a South African connection, maybe through the Chequers Bank in Cape Town, managed for years by guy called Larry Lauderdale."

The Thrill of a Crop Sprayer

In The Air From Jozi to Easthope

"Sorry, Rosy, it took a while with Bruce, reducing juicy facts to a half page of nothingness, well, getting agreement. I was hoping we might have had lunch."

"Actually, I had a sandwich with Peter."

"How was poncy?"

"Tim, I think you need help. Peter was charming. Why did you boil the facts down to nothing?"

"The collective thinking is that we should give Atwell the impression he's safe, and hopefully he'll dismiss any thoughts of applying for amnesty."

"And thereby not escape the long arm of Joshua Chios' law. Nice plane."

"NO, this way." I said.

Rosy had spotted an executive four-seater aircraft, but after hearing me and turning, she stopped in her tracks, gawping.

"What the hell is that? It doesn't even have a roof."

"Canopy."

"Tim, it doesn't matter what the fuck it's called, it doesn't have one."

"Beautiful, isn't it? Very rare, an open-topped, two-seater crop sprayer. It'll take off and land anywhere. Give me your bag. It'll jam in against the insecticide tank."

"Oh, for Christ's sake."

"I'll give you a hand up; take the back seat, obviously. Here are some goggles, and a hat with aircom, plugs in on the right. Make sure the door's closed and your seat belt is really tight. If you fall out you'll get cross."

"Bugger off. I flew you Upper Class to London and back, and you're taking me up in a bright yellow kit plane without a roof, with nothing to see but the back of your head."

"You'll be able to look at the ground when I turn

you upside down."

"I do hope you're joking me."

"Rosy, if you feel your nervousness about being in this aircraft needs feeding, bear in mind this beautiful croppy belongs to Schwartz. It was parked in the same hanger as my old plane – you could be sitting on a bomb."

"Shut up."

Twenty minutes into the flight Rosy's mood was entirely transformed.

"Tim, this is fantastic." She said.

It was necessary to shout through the aircom radio connection, our words were modulating in sync with the croppy's pulsing engine.

"There's nothing like it. Ready for a bit of fun?"

"I suppose, but take it easy."

It's almost impossible to stall a croppy – a combination of its wingspan and engine power. I pulled back on the joystick and we entered a steep climb. A minute or so later after crossing the escarpment face our height above the ground increased to three-and-a-half thousand feet and the world fell away beneath us. I levelled out and pushed the joystick in the opposite direction, fully forward.

We began roaring towards the ground, accelerating to a speed the likes of which Rosy had never known. The noise level doubled and redoubled. The air tore past our ears and I could vaguely hear some sketchy screaming. At fifteen hundred feet I pulled back on the stick and the croppy's nose shot up like the unoccupied end of a seesaw. The plane's fuselage moved in an instant to become vertical and rushed upwards. Rosy's body was compressed and spread over her seat, causing her safety harness straps to hang slack across her when the croppy began falling on its back at the start of a loop's top arc. We both absorbed the reality of being upside down and loose. The G-forces flattened the flesh in our cheeks and our bodies, a touch too much for Rosy stomach which oozed a bialy secretion into the back of her throat.

The croppy was inverted for four seconds as it followed the loop's circular route through the air, and while Rosy hung upside down she gripped with such power that the seat frame drew blood from her fingers. Not that I knew at the time but four seconds was long enough for the contents of Rosy's throat to flow into her mouth and induce a bout of vomiting, messily expelling Peter Lipscombe's lunch-time offering.

After easing the croppy off the lower arc and back into level flight I began shouting with exhilaration.

"AMAZING. THAT WAS AMAZING."

There wasn't a word from the back, just a spitting, spluttering noise, after which Rosy pulled a tissue from her pocket and wiped her face.

"AMAZING. WHAT D'YOU THINK?"

Rosy ignored me a second time as she dabbed tissue around the cockpit, collecting the small pieces of her technicoloured yawn.

"Rosy?"

And she continued to ignore me.

"Rosy, are you all right? Talk to me. Did you enjoy that?"

You bastard, you BASTARD.

"Rosy?"

"You're DEAD. I'll do Smit's work for him."

∞

A croppy's stall speed is so slow that we virtually hopped onto the runway, at Easthope, allowing me to take the first taxi exit to the hangers. After cutting the engine and waiting a short while as the prop slowed to a halt, we climbed down over the wing. When my feet hit the ground Rosy leant forward, cupped a hand behind my head and pulled my face firmly towards hers, connecting our lips with a determined strength. It was then that I realised what had happened, but too late, and I was held squirming for release until Rosy decided enough was enough.

"My God, yuk, that's disgusting. What the hell did Lipscombe give you for lunch?"

Rosy beamed a self-satisfied smile as we walked to return Schwartz's GPS.

"How are you fixed for getting home?" I said.

"I'm fine, dad's picking me up. How do those things work?"

"GPS stands for global positioning satellite. Look, it's easy. You switch it on here, you have to wait a few moments for it to calibrate, there we go. Now, basically it's picking up signals from satellites, and by computing the information it can tell you where you are, and amazingly accurately, and if you move it can tell what direction you're moving in and it can calculate your speed. It also stores destinations. It can fly an aircraft automatically when it's interfaced with the autopilot – it handles the entire navigation. If we were flying back to Jozi right now, we'd punch in Jo to the location memory, there we are Jozi, and the plane would take us there – no pilot. And just for interest, the location following Jozi, press the down arrow. Shit!"

"What?"

"Jungle Junction. Shit, it's Schwartz's GPS, so he's flown Jungle Junction, and recently – this model isn't even two years old. You remember, Zambezi Trekkers, Jungle Junction."

A Digital Rat

Easthope

"Hi Rosy, you look great." Oliver said

"Thanks Dad."

"Hey, you sounded mysterious on the phone, tell me what's happening. Why on earth do you want to meet Jordan Atwell?"

"I've discovered he's as evil as they come. You never much liked him, did you."

"I didn't dislike him, and working with him as a regional director for Pan African Commerce had its moments of fun, but he was never going to be a soul mate. Evil's a strong word."

"I tell you, Atwell's a perfectly superfluous piece of humanity."

"Nice, so why have I invited Jordan de Atwell-Evil to dinner tonight, other than to indulge my daughter's devil-busting instincts?"

"Okay, to begin with, he's amassed an illegal fortune at the expense of thousands of victims, most of whom are dead."

∞

"Larry Lauderdale speaking."

"Larry, it's Jordan Atwell. Theo gave me your message last week, said to organise a transfer. Is it ready?"

"It's taken longer this month, shuffling the funds through enough accounts to cover our tracks. Later tonight – I suggest you handle it first thing tomorrow."

"How much, roughly?"

"About $185m."

"Not bad for a month's takings."

"Justifies a beer or two. Are you in town tonight?"

"Unfortunately, no. I'll be back but not until the small hours. Just arrived in Easthope, parked up outside The View, about to have an early braai with the Lennox family."

"Keeping up appearances?"

"Exactly. Oliver's daughter has asked for some careers advice, she's thinking of returning to South Africa.

Larry, I think it's time to get out. I'll talk it through with you tomorrow but I've just had a disturbing conversation with Theo, explaining Smit's recent lack of success. The little shit decided to set up on his own, which as far as I'm concerned is the exact same thing as asking for a bullet to pass through your frontal lobe. He did a deal with Taylor and the Kimbos, let the bastards escape in exchange for a large amount of our money."

"Really?"

"Yeah, really. Also, now he's demanding a share of the offshore kitty."

"How did he even know about it?"

"God knows. Anyway, Theo is playing him along and Gillmor's getting ready to take the bastard out, and I don't mean romantically.

"I'll make the transfer first thing."

"Enjoy the braai, Jordan."

∞

"Try this voluptuous chardonnay. Atwell is here, parked up outside, talking on his mobile. I signalled to him to come through when he's finished. Did you have a good flight down with Tim?"

"Not so much down as upside down, he looped a croppy, forced a re-acquaintance with my lunch."

"Messy. Rosy, quite a story you told me, I've often wondered about Atwell's loot."

"And you've not heard the half of it yet, I'll tell you more later. Anyway, Dad, you're clear about what to do?"

"I think so."

"The main thing is to get him away from the laptop before Tim rings to distract him, and then keep him away. I'll need just over a minute to unzip the file and load the spyware, not long but it's essential he doesn't see what I'm doing. Listen, it's life threateningly essential, this is serious stuff."

"Christ, I've got it, I don't know why but I've got it."

"Good, I'll give you the nod."

∞

"Jordan, nice to see you. My daughter, Rosy."

"Hello, Oliver. Pleased to see you again Rosy. I saw you at the wedding but the last time we spoke, umm, years ago."

"Mr. Atwell, good evening."

"Please, call me Jordan."

"Okay. Jordan, thanks very much for coming over this evening. I really appreciate it, and for bringing the database along. Well, I assume you brought your laptop?"

"Yes, of course."

"That's marvellous."

"Jordan, what can I get you?"

"I'd like a Campari, ice, slice of orange, that would be great, thanks.

"Rosy, I'm only too pleased to be able to help, although I don't have an upbeat view of housing associations. In the last few years they've spent billions building trash homes to house trash people. Those wasters should get off their ethnic backsides and build their own houses, buy their own land for that matter.

Buy it back, maybe. Your thieving mates stole their smallholdings in the first place with the Native Land Act.

"We should do the listing now? Get it out of the way before we eat."

"Good idea," Rosy said.

"Jordan, it's easier to set up inside, after you."

Atwell opened his laptop on a table under a portrait of Laura Lennox.

"Your mother was a beautiful woman." He said.

Your victim was a beautiful woman.

"It was a tragedy, inexplicable, contracting a strain of anthrax so virulent that it killed her within hours, and Lilly of course, our maid. I read that the nearest outbreak of anthrax at the time was two thousand miles away in Zimbabwe."

"Yes, I remember. I was in Harare around that time." Atwell said.

"Jordan, did you know the particular strain of anthrax in that outbreak wasn't indigenous to Zimbabwe, it was imported, some say."

"I didn't know that, no."

Lying bastard, you delivered it.

"The community affected realised a biological

agent had been used against them."

Shit, Rosy that's too much detail. Be careful.

She turned her gaze to Atwell's chubby fingers. A second earlier and she would have seen him enter the whole of what she assumed to be his user ID, as it was she caught the last three characters and a row of asterisks as the dialogue box faded from the screen.

"Rosy, how did you learn of such things?"

Smiling at Atwell, Rosy was inwardly slapping herself for such a bolshie lack of control and wondering how to answer.

"I spent some time with Tim Kitson, sneaked a look, not that he knows, at his research papers."

Atwell looked up slowly from his laptop.

"Do you think the people responsible will ever be caught?" He said.

Bet your fucking life you will.

"I doubt it, strangely, there are no names. The people responsible are in the clear."

"Really? Oh, here we are, housing associations."

"Jordan, I'll just use the bathroom before we get started," Rosy said.

"Tim, you've got two minutes." Rosy said.

Having rung me from the loo she then gave Oliver the nod, who grabbed a bowl of biltong and Atwell's Campari and followed Rosy back to the conservatory.

"Jordan," he said, "let's take these nibbles and our drinks outside. We can stoke the braai and catch up while Rosy browses the information you've brought along."

"Okay, Oliver."

"Is this your mobile, Jordan?" Oliver asked, scooping it on to the tray.

"Rosy, let me know if you need any help." Atwell said.

"Thanks Jordan,"

Rosy turned with a nervous energy to his laptop.

Even before Atwell's feet hit the patio Rosy's right hand clicked through the start menu, opened the explore utility and navigated to the computer's external drive. There was an audible clunk as the drive accepted Rosy's disc and began reading it, and a series of whirring clicks as the machine obeyed instructions to run and install.

"Atwell speaking," Rosy heard from the patio, as the data began its transfer.

"Jordan, I'll nip in and grab the meat." Oliver said.

"Everything okay, Rosy?" He whispered.

"Yes but stay out there, keep him occupied."

"He's on the phone."

"I know that! But you have to keep him out there."

"Mr. Atwell, we spoke last week. You were interested in the front companies associated with Project Costa."

"You have some information, Mr. Kitson?"

"You were concerned that certain companies might receive a bad press if they were involved in the chemical and biological supply chain. I'm ringing to allay your fears; nobody, in or out of Government, has the slightest inclination to pursue such things. Even if they had the energy, the reports are bereft of names, those responsible are in the clear."

Atwell listened to me but began to move and he re-entered the conservatory.

"That's very interesting," he said.

He cast a glance in Rosy's direction as he continued to talk.

"Mr. Kitson, you're not the first person to have said that to me today."

Oliver moved away from Rosy as Atwell crossed the conservatory's threshold, and having assessed the situation Oliver moved quickly with the braai meats and left Atwell no polite option other than to retreat back onto the patio in order to let Oliver pass.

The laptop's screen displayed a transfer window with thirty-five seconds remaining. After Oliver passed, Atwell manoeuvred forward and stepped back into the conservatory. Rosy smiled gently at him to acknowledge his presence, but her head was screaming for Oliver.

How will I eject the disc without Atwell seeing?

As Atwell stepped towards her, Rosy instinctively turned the screen, unobtrusively but to an angle that inhibited his view. With twenty-one seconds remaining Atwell was on top of her as she stood to obscure the transfer window, but not before pressing speed dial three on her mobile.

"Sorry? No, that's okay..." Atwell, said, "Mr. Kitson, if it's an urgent call put me on hold for a moment. I'll collect my beer from the patio."

"Jordan, would you mind topping up my chardonnay while you're there? Thank you." Rosy said.

Atwell turned towards the patio with six seconds remaining. As he left the conservatory there was an audible bleep from his laptop, together with a screen message confirming the successful installation of Rosy's RAT (Remote Access Trojan), the arcane digital equivalent of a salivating bloodhound.

Rosy ejected the disc with one hand and grabbed up her mobile with the other.

"Tim, are you still there?"

"Yes, what do you want?"

"Nothing. Thanks!"

Rosy's Mother

The View

"Thank God he's gone."

"You were going to tell more – Atwell's dark side."

"You're not going to like it. Pour yourself a stiff one."

"If you insist." Oliver said.

"Cheers."

"Cheers, Daddy. Well, Atwell built up a financial war chest that was formidable. A combination of siphoned revenues, commissions, and covert funding. Then, in collusion with the Government, he took advantage of a volatile gold market and pocketed $2 billion."

"Billion! Good God."

"He used the money to finance Recce cross border raids and to fund a huge drug manufacturing operation. According to the CIA he's trafficking narcotics across the entire continent."

"Amazing." Oliver said.

"Although Atwell himself began as a Recce, operating in Angola and Mozambique, after that he became director of Project Costa and was responsible for South Africa's chemical and biological warfare programme.

"Do you remember, around the time Mum and Lilly died, there was an outbreak of anthrax in Zimbabwe. Well, there's no longer any doubt that the bacteria was supplied to Zimbabwe by South Africa, in other words by Atwell."

"Bacillus anthracis." Oliver said.

"Yes. What else do you remember?"

"Lots, it's capable of producing spores, with protective casings that allow them to survive for years. Enters the body through the skin or the lungs, and that's the most dangerous, through the lungs, pulmonary anthrax. Yet, strangely, it's not contagious, it's transmission depends on exposure rather than one person spreading it to another."

"Which in the history of what happened here is odd, isn't it? It means Mum and Lilly were both exposed, and without leaving Easthope."

"Where are you taking me?" Oliver said.

"Nowhere good, but it's a worthwhile journey. Remember anything else?"

"Well, it produces itchy lumps that swell, and after a while they ulcerate and form black scabs, hence anthrax, the Greek word for coal."

"The day mother and Lilly died, Atwell was here in the morning, visiting on business. He did a lot of shouting, Emma and I were still young but he accused us of taking something from his briefcase on the kitchen table. At the time he didn't say what."

"I remember that, surprisingly, given what else happened that day, he was in a real flap."

"Do you remember what the police found in Lilly's hand?"

"Ah, her liniment bottle? For her carbuncles?"

"Yes. Carbuncle Juice is what it said on the bottle. Daddy, the anthrax lumps, their characteristic appearance, they look like carbuncles. I was with the CIA in Washington yesterday, they showed me a file on Project Costa. Guess what their code-name was for the anthrax agent."

"Shit."

"Yes, they called it Carbuncle Juice. Lilly complained about her feet from dawn 'til dusk. She must have snuck the Carbuncle Juice from Atwell's briefcase, taking it at face value."

"Holy fuck... Atwell killed Laura?"

Catch Up Time

Easthope

Next morning I caught up with Rosy to confirm our return flight from Easthope to Jozi was on schedule.

"I'll see you at the private departures gate. How did it go with Atwell last night?"

"Okay, but the man's nasty. I told Dad about the Carbuncle Juice. He was pretty upset."

"I can imagine."

"But we did it, the spy software is on his laptop and gathering information as we speak. Karl rang earlier to say Atwell was online."

"Banking?"

"Not yet, just collecting emails."

"But everything's working?"

"Yeah, thanks to Karl. I've arranged to meet him at Lipscombes, later this morning."

"If you have lunch with Poncy, it's over." I said.

"Really? And what sanction would you impose if I have sex with him?"

"Shut up. Listen, sorry I didn't make it over last night, I ended up having a few beers with Schwartz, didn't finish until late."

"What did he have to say?"

"Basically, he's not involved. He acted as an air taxi and apparently he knows Jungle Junction like the back of his hand. He's even offered to help us out if we need him. Oh, and the GPS, the coordinates were an automatic download from the previous model; hasn't been there in years."

"That's good news, Tim."

"Rosy, I had a chat with Andrew this morning. He's agreed to an interview on the record. Hopefully, I'll scratch out the first few paragraphs of my world exclusive. I've booked a Cape Town flight, also late morning, around the same time you're off to Poncy."

"Okay, see you in a while at check-in."

Constantia Nek

At home in Constantia Nek, in the posh residential hills of Cape Town, Jordan Atwell was relating his own version of the previous evening.

"How was Oliver Lennox?" Theo said.

"Oliver was okay, but his daughter, Rosy, she's barking. Has a notion to build a few million houses for the squatting township blacks. Where does she think the money's coming from? The Government can barely pay its bar tab.

"While I was there Tim Kitson called, said nobody's named and little was going to happen. The heat's off. Even so, it's time we pulled the plug."

"Everything's in place," Theo said.

"Okay. While I organise the transfer, have a word with Larry and get him to come over, we'll make a plan. And tell me, Theo, how is Smit leaving the planet?"

"I spoke to him last night, cheeky bastard, wanted to know if I'd decided on his share of the offshore monies. Anyway, I gave him the impression Kitson is lying low at Gravelotte, told him to rendezvous with Gillmor this morning, which he thought was unnecessary, but he's unaware of exactly what Gillmor has in mind for him."

Bazaruto

Moses was also catching up, ringing Jabu in Bazaruto from Cape Town.

"Hi, Naomi, what the hell's that racket?"

"Hi, Moses, did you have a good trip?" Naomi said.

"Yes, fine. We're off to see Andrew in a moment. Thought I'd have a quick word with Jabu. What the hell's going on there?"

"It's a huge celebration; I reckon the whole island's

here."

"What you celebrating?"

"I'll let Jabu tell you."

"Put him on."

"Hang on. JABU," Naomi shouted.

"PUT THE SAXOPHONE DOWN. IT'S MOSES."

"Saxophone, Naomi?" Moses said.

"Yes, that's the good news. We went to Vilanculos. Jabu kept the broken teeth pieces, so big the dentist managed to pin and glue 'em together. Jabu bought a dented saxophone, but it sounds great."

"Naomi, what d'you mean, good news?"

"Here's Jabu. Be well."

"Hi Moses."

"Jabu, what going on there? Sounds like the Madi Gras, amplified."

"Moses, I got my teeth fixed."

"Naomi said."

"Moses, can you hear everybody celebrating?"

"Course I can."

"Everybody's happy."

"Naomi mentioned the good news, teeth and all. So what's the bad news?"

"That is the bad news, everybody being happy."

"How come?"

"Badgers. In the archipelago they bring good luck."

"What the hell are you talking about?"

"Nobody knows where this one came from, but when it turned up people began following it about. Early this morning half the island were sat watching it root around in the sand dunes. It was gonna bring them luck, good fortune, so they stayed with it."

"What's so special about this badger?"

"Well, this badger, Moses, this badger,"

"Spit it out, Jabu."

"This badger is a honey badger."

"HONEY..." Moses bellowed.

"The islanders shared the money between

'emselves, the money in the honey container...

"A HONEY BADGER!"

"Moses,"

There was a knock on the hotel room door.

"JESUS CHRIST, JABU."

Moses slammed the phone down and opened the door.

"What's up?" Stefan said.

"It's family, don't let's go there."

"Okay."

"Did you get through to Emma?" Moses said.

"She's fine. Apparently Kitson's bush chalet is idyllic, but isolated, the nearest shop's twenty miles off in Mulati. There's a houseboy-cum-night watchman and an over-affectionate nanny goat, but that's it!"

"Least she's not plagued by honey badgers."

"Ah, no. Shall we go see Andrew?"

Cape Town

"Stefan, what you describe is unbelievable. Nerve agents are bad enough, but throwing half-paralysed soldiers into the sea from a thousand feet, it's hardly Geneva Convention stuff." Andrew said.

Andrew shook his head for a few moments.

"That's amazing too," he said, "the fact you were at Kassinga together, well, not together, on opposite sides, but you know what I mean."

"Stefan," Moses said, "I never understood Kassinga, so many women and children."

"Same way Recces never understood your boys jumping the border to rape white farmers' wives and their daughters."

"It was crazy. My cousin Nancy, she was raped, and then murdered by Smit."

"Smit?" Stefan said.

"Shot her in the head while she was snuggled up like a baby."

"Jesus."

"Moses, Stefan, thanks for testifying. I've been admitting evidence for two years; you've slipped in on the last day, cutting it a bit fine, but thanks. And the people you've identified, it's perfect timing, you've exposed them, but they are rightly out of time."

"Sure thing. Andrew, long time since Ethiopia," Moses said.

"Yeah, long time. Do you still see the Mandoba brothers?"

The question caused Stefan to stir, to fidget, and he turned towards Moses in anticipation of an answer.

"Frank and Georgie both died. Their family didn't hear anything for a couple of years, then out of the blue they gets a photograph through the post, no letter, just the picture. Frank and Georgie was lying rigid, a bullet between the eyes, and, oh fuck, their hearts, their hearts cut out."

Stefan grabbed the waste bin.

Stefan's mostly ineffectual retches and a small rush of greenish fluid forced Andrew and Moses to look at him.

"I still have nightmares."

"About Frank and Georgie?" Moses said.

"It was disgusting. It was Smit again, psychopathic bastard."

"Stefan, stay calm. Take it easy, tell us what happened." Andrew said.

"OK. Moses, there was an organisation called the Urban Foundation, it promoted programmes to ease social deprivation. There was a time when they disseminated information by deploying the army in rural locations in a variety of community schemes, all designed to win the hearts and minds of the blacks, the WHAM strategy.

"Smit turned it into a sick joke.

"He arrested Frank and Georgie attempting to blow up a power line near Barberton, had them staked out on the ground in a nearby spruce plantation. Jesus, Moses, I'm sorry. I should have done something, but they were all into it, all of them. Smit leant over them and said he didn't think he'd ever win their hearts and minds, so he'd simply take their hearts. And that's what the bastard did, cut out their hearts as they breathed, threw them twitching into the vegetation."

Puppet On a String

Gravelotte

Kipling wrote of the great grey-green, greasy Limpopo River, all set about with fever trees, in his book The Elephant's Child. About the same time as he wrote, a self-seeded fever tree parked itself in the grounds of what eventually became my bush-hut on the banks of that greasy river. During the Friday morning that Emma drove to Mulati to stock up on essentials, and tethered to that very same fever tree was a lonesome nanny goat. The approach of humans always caused her to bleat excitedly, which is what she was doing as Michael the houseboy walked towards her rattling a bucket, intent on milk.

Twenty-five metres away, hidden and silent in the tall savannah grass, Smit contracted his body – a reflex, as if to shrink beyond the visible. Motionless, he watched Michael work the goat's teats, listening to the squirting ring as milk hit the bucket's rim. He should have been further back from the house, anticipating his rendezvous with Gillmor, but Smit's highly adrenalised body had refused to stir. He was there to kill, and he recognised a familiar enthusiasm. His emotions were scatty, his surface-level thinking consumed by a sadistic vision, a component of Smit's life instinct that produced a surge of libido. Watching Michael's hands squeeze and pull the teats, the thought of ejaculating crept into Smit's thinking. He unzipped his trousers and masturbated, sending several long strings of semen into the grass as he twitched to the milk's rhythmic splatter on the bucket's rim.

A little later he began to crawl off to rendezvous with Gillmor, but he heard an approaching vehicle and froze. Smit watched a blue Volkswagen park up and its driver's door swing open. Through binoculars he watched the driver walk to its boot and collect her shopping.

What's she doing here?

Smit studied Emma's feminine form through a magnification factor of eight, moving his voyeuristic eyes from her lips to her breasts and back again. He imagined parts of her body he couldn't see, and he imagined kissing her, somehow with Emma's consent. He was consumed by a second libidinous surge, an unstoppable compulsion, and he crept forward through the grass to its edge. Watching Emma disappear inside was a frustration, and caused him to make a dash for the fever tree, startling the goat as he crashed against its trunk to conceal himself. Yet the goat wasn't startled for long, and it began bleating and licking, bringing Emma to the kitchen window in an attempt to understand the commotion. Yet Smit moved unseen to the cover of a purple-flowering hibiscus.

Smit's aching tautness summoned an anarchic power, lechery bore into him with a poisoned energy, mobilising him without compassion from the hibiscus to the kitchen to the lounge, where he threw Emma down on a sofa.

"What do you want?" Emma said.

"You."

"Smit, no. No! You bastard, get off me. GET OFF ME."

"Emma, you'd better stop fighting."

Smit was strong and he held Emma's lips against his own with one hand, and he was quick to sidestep Emma's knee as it jerked upwards towards his groin. For him it was erotic, although the pain of Emma's fingernails slowly tearing his face was too much, causing him to thwack her with the butt end of his pistol.

Emma crumpled from the impact, her legs jelly-like as the gun butt scrambled her brain.

"Stand up." Smit said.

"FUCK OFF YOU BASTARD, LET GO OF ME."

Yet Smit held on, pulling Emma forward at the same time as thrusting his right hand and its thick fingers between her legs. In defence Emma went for his face again, but with both hands – four nails a side ripping deep into his fleshy cheeks, an excoriation that not even the Smit could endure. He punched her, reducing Emma to a wobbler who fell into his arms.

He lay her face down across the sofa, her head buried in the cushions on the far side of the armrest. He stood there, motionless and gawping, the kitchen window at his back streaming sunlight to illuminate the unfolding horror. Positioned at her rear he used both hands to lift the hem of Emma's short red skirt, before loosening his clothing and allowing it to hit the floor.

Outside, beneath the fever tree, the nanny goat lay dead in a rich-red pool of its own blood. Its throat had been slit from ear to ear by Gillmor – he had watched Smit's progress and was allowing no chance of a bleating advertisement of his own arrival.

Emma came round and began to struggle, and there to watch from the far side of the hibiscus was Gillmor.

"Stay still." Smit said.

Emma twisted violently to one side, and in a way that momentarily exposed her face.

Gillmor screamed her name in desperation, raised his gun and squeezed the trigger. In that instant Smit both turned his upper body to the sound of Gillmor's voice and took a bullet through the side of his skull. The bullet's velocity lifted Smit's whole body, throwing it forwards across the sofa, where it slumped down over Emma, skidding on a little towards her shoulders. A thick fountain of blood pulsed rhythmically from Smit's temple, and his gun hand crumpled beneath him as he crashed across Emma's back.

Before Smit's body came to a complete stop his index finger created a precarious pressure on his gun's trigger. Gillmor heard the shot as he stepped through the kitchen towards the lounge, where he pulled Smit's half-naked body off Emma and threw it to the floor. Yet it wasn't until he adjusted Emma's skirt and composed himself that he saw the neat hole to the left side of her spine. The bullet had entered through Emma's back and travelled on through her heart and left breast, taking itself deep into the sofa's upholstery. Gillmor leant forward to confirm Emma's death, and finding no pulse he stood upright to empty his gun into Smit, mostly into Smit's torso but three bullets tore away his damp and once lascivious penis.

Gillmor fell to his knees. In tears he hugged Emma's body. For years his feelings for had existed only from a distance, but that made them no less real, and he felt the pain of this single death. Two minutes passed before he registered the danger to him of his presence there, and then he fled.

Smit's death held no pain for Gillmor, nor reward,

it was simply disappointing. Smit was a psychopath, of course, yet this was a second rate closure for Gillmor – he had shot up a puppet. Wet uncoagulated blood was all over the place, but it was nothing more than a puppet's stuffing. The guy who pulled the strings was the mover, the Boss-man was the rapist.

The Power of Zero & One

Jozi

Rosy strolled into Peter Lipscombe's office feeling driven – she could soon have the financial wherewithal for changing thousands of ordinary township lives.

"Morning Peter, Karl. I'm really excited. Karl, does Peter know he's employed an IT guru of cosmic stature?"

"I have told him, but to be honest, when it goes beyond a double mouse click they're a bit slow around here, particularly Peter."

"Cheeky bugger, but you're right. In fact, if it's okay with you two, I'll sit in on what you're doing for a bit. Educate me and I'll buy you lunch."

"It's a deal." Rosy said.

"Okay, let's go crack some code," Peter said.

"Keystroke encryption."

"Thanks Karl, okay, let's go crack some keystroke encryption."

The three of them sped downwards for seven floors, before walking a long corridor to the bank's data processing area, chatting, joking, and catching up.

"Karl, when we first met, you were an anarchic scriptkiddy. Look at you now!"

"Rosy, we all grow up."

"Scriptkiddy?" Peter said.

"Teenage computer geek. A cross between a sideshow performer who bites the heads off live animals and a virtual villain. Out to get all large corporations, dead or alive."

As they reached the IT suite, Karl hit the electronic door lock and gestured Rosy to go ahead. The environment was similar to Daryl's CIA facility in Washington, an IT wonderland of groundbreaking technology and blistering computer power.

"Over here. Grab a seat. Bear with."

Karl keyed in a password and his desktop pinged to life as he dialled an internal number.

"Hi, Keith I'm back on station, I'll take over.

Anything happened? Okay, thanks."

He replaced the receiver and double-clicked the RAT icon.

"RAT?" Peter said.

"Remote Access Trojan." Karl said.

"Before you can crack encrypted transactions sent over the internet, you need some method of intercepting the data in the first place. A Remote Access Trojan is a malicious computer program that does just that, it's also simply called a Trojan, you know, Trojan Horse.

"Rosy did the intrepid stuff, installing it directly on to Atwell's laptop without him knowing. Now, great news. Fabio & Nicholson are still using 40bit encryption and not the new 128bit."

"The new 128bit encryption is three times as powerful, yeah?" Peter said.

"Ah, not quite. Do you know what a bit is?" Rosy said.

"Not really."

"Okay, it's short for binary digit, and obviously there are only two. A bit represents either 0 or 1, so each bit gives you a choice of two. Now, 40bit encryption is two to the fortieth power, about a billion! So, 128bit is the 40bit number, a billion, doubled over and over on itself another eighty-eight times."

"Jesus!" Peter said.

"So, searching all the possible keystrokes using a single computer would take years. Some people reckon cracking a 128bit encryption that way would take considerably longer than the age of the universe. So, it's far easier to install spyware, such as our Trojan. If that's not a hundred percent we can still hack in and deal with things in the old way, with a little brute force, trying trillions of keystroke combinations until we find one that works, but obviously not with a single computer, which is why Karl has lined up several hundred to run in parallel, should we need them." Rosy said.

"Has it been done, Karl, cracking it that way?" Peter said.

"Yeah, but it took six days."

"Amazing. Karl, how did you gain access to so many

computers?"

"You just need to know the right people, or be in the right environment."

"And who might the right people be?" Peter said.

"Well, IT managers, bank managers, that sort of person."

"Jesus! Let me see if I understand you properly. My branch ATMs stop dispensing cash for six days, while you access their processing power. Is that the idea?"

"Peter, don't worry, Karl's very competent, and he wouldn't let that happen." Rosy said.

"Okay, let's see what we've got. Atwell was online earlier this morning, and went online again about twenty minutes ago, sent a couple of emails, but as yet, no banking. I just spoke with Keith, he said it was a bit scary earlier when Atwell opened a spyware scanner, but for whatever reason he didn't initiate a scan."

"Will he see us if he does that, Karl?"

"Probably, but not necessarily. Peter, it depends on his spyware scanner – on an automatic setting it would scan the memory and the registry, and then check the cookies folder for anything dangerous. Well, we're hidden among the files, so it just depends.

Karl opened a connection to Atwell's computer and all three fell silent as they watched an Atwell's aquatic screensaver – the red snappers and angelfish were extraordinarily colourful, and mildly hypnotic.

"Peter, what we don't want to do here is to disturb Atwell's computer screen, we need to operate in the background. If the fish stop swimming and his laptop starts moving its own cursor he might become suspicious."

"Just a bit, Karl." Rosy said.

Cape Town

"The computer's up and running but I'm waiting on the bank to start trading, thirty minutes to go." Atwell said.

"Jordan, I've talked with Larry, he'll be over in about an hour, but I've not heard from Gillmor yet. I'll be in the ops room if you need me." Theo said.

Theo headed inside as the Lipscombes team connected to Atwell's aquatic screen saver, before instigating a search. When Karl clicked the Trojan icon from a 1000 miles away a green light flickered in Theo's peripheral vision from Atwell's laptop. He took a look and assumed, largely because of the miniaturised icon in the taskbar, that Jordan had instigated a spyware search.

Jozi

"Brilliant." Karl said.

The search results scrolled down his screen.

"Twenty-two files and a cookie!"

Karl clicked open the first, and then almost immediately the second, and then the third, and so on, making it obvious he could ascertain content with a cursory glance.

"Nothing very special, but I'll print the bank's contact sheet, there's a list of the personnel, names, job titles, telephone numbers."

Between Jozi & Constantia Nek

Karl gently touched Rosy's shoulder and pointed to the computer screen, they watched together as Atwell's browser opened to its home page.

∞

"We're going banking," Karl said.

They watched together as Atwell open a drop down menu and clicked the Fabio & Nicholson link.

"Fantastic." Rosy said.

∞

"Did you get through to Gillmor?"

"No, I dare say he'll ring in later." Theo said.

∞

"Did the spyware scan clean?" Theo said.

"I haven't done that yet. I was going to earlier, but got distracted."

"But I saw it running. Look, the shortcut icon, it's still in the taskbar. Jordan, open it and just check when it last completed a scan."

∞

"Shit, they've opened the spyware scanner." Karl

said.

∞

"A week ago. It hasn't been running today." Atwell said.

"But I saw it running." Theo said.

Atwell clicked the login logo for business banking and arrived at the password and user ID screen. He positioned his cursor over the password box while Theo stood puzzling things. But then, after Atwell began to type, and the RAT programme retrieved the first few characters, causing another flickering of the laptop's green light, Theo was immediately suspicious.

"Jordan, stop. Disconnect." He said.

Karl read the characters that appeared before him, JJ 35.

"What's up?" Atwell said.

"I'm not sure, but disconnect, immediately."

∞

"Shit, they've gone off-line." Rosy said.

"Don't worry; to make the transaction they'll have to come back, and we'll be here." Karl said.

∞

"Jordan, there's something strange here, too much background activity. Before you go back online, log on to our local network, I'll use my PC to look at what's happening on your laptop. When you're back online do exactly what you did before, get to the point of typing the first four characters and then pull the plug. It'll look as if there's a recurring problem."

It took a few moments for Atwell to log on with the local network and for Theo to boot up his machine and open a connection.

"Okay, I'm ready. Jordan, don't go straight to Fabio & Nicholson, log on but then let the laptop stand idle, I'll tell you when to proceed."

Theo initiated a spyware scan and then clicked open the local network's task manager. He moved through its options to select the performance window, and after Atwell's machine was allowed to stand idle, Theo monitored its processing unit's activity graph in the performance window. The usage fell and settled at around two percent, telling him there was no other programme active at that time.

∞

"They're back." Rosy said.

"Great! I've disabled the auto retrieve, we'll watch rather than gather, and try to confirm we haven't been spotted."

∞

"Okay, Jordan, connect with the bank as before, but only the first four keyboard characters, no more, in case they can be read."

As Jordan Atwell began navigating to Fabio & Nicholson's website, and Karl and Rosy glued themselves to their screen in anticipation, Theo began a keyboard interrogation of his own. A few moments later Atwell interacted with the password screen and then shouted across the room.

"Disconnecting."

"Okay, and then reconnect as soon as you like." Theo said.

Theo was fully absorbed with the columns of base sixteen, hexadecimal notation scrolling before him.

∞

"Oh shit, they're off-line again." Rosy said.

"That's interesting, exactly the same point as they'd reached last time, same four characters of the password. I don't think they're on to us; it's just a glitch. Next time we'll reconnect and gather some data." Karl said.

Rosy gave Karl a nod and returned to Fabio & Nicholson's contact sheet. The Assistant Manager was G F McCall.

Do I know him? No. And the Marketing Manager, K M Warrington, Security, I D Isherwood. Do I know them? No.

"God, they're back again. Fingers crossed." Karl said.

∞

"Fuck." Theo said.

Karl's computer reconnected automatically and Atwell's processing activity shot up to eighty three per cent.

"What's up?" Atwell said.

"They're here this time, whoever they are,

interrogating your computer."

"Fucking bastards," Atwell said.

"Jordan, I smell a RAT." Theo said.

A few seconds later while Atwell was navigating to the British Virgin Islands a third time, there was a series of bleeps and pings from Theo's PC. The spyware scanner had found the RAT, and Theo's military decryption app had quarantined Karl's reconnecting pulse, analysed it and thrown up the location data.

Larry Lauderdale entered the room to hear Theo shouting.

"I thought so, but Jordan, how the fuck did it get on your machine?"

"I haven't a clue. Shall I disconnect again?"

"No, leave it open, but no input, I'll take it over from here."

Theo cut and pasted the location data and clicked go.

"Who the fuck are Lipscombes? Hang on, it's a bank. Jordan, you're being interrogated by a bank. Larry, do you know Lipscombes?"

"Yes I do, and there's a very obvious connection. The chairman is Peter Lipscombe, who just happens to be a close friend of Rosy Lennox, who just happens to be the person Jordan had dinner with last night."

"Fuck it! I left her alone with my computer thinking she was a bimbo."

∞

"Shit." Karl said

"What's our home page doing on their computer?

While Karl pondered his own Lipscombes' logo, Theo typed FUCK OFF across the screen in a twenty-eight point font.

"Christ! How did he do that, at that speed?" Karl said.

Karl hastily sent a bloodhound cookie before severing the connection.

"Bollocks. I expected better, sorry, Rosy. We have four characters of their password but that's about it for the moment."

"Not entirely, I have the last three characters of

their user ID."

"Really?"

"Yeah, I saw Atwell key them in yesterday."

"What are they?"

"149."

"Great, we're almost there, I don't think. But we do have an invitation to lunch."

"Let's go," Rosy said.

∞

"Jesus, Jordan. That was close, very close." Theo said.

"Too close," Larry said.

"You know, I thought Kitson was just a bit too helpful when he rang last night at the Lennoxes', a bit too fucking polite, they're obviously in it together. It's time to fuck off boys.

"Theo, the sooner you raise Gillmor the better. Have him mobilise the team for dawn, including sleepers. I want at least a hundred men, and let's work with an ETA of midday tomorrow at Jungle Junction. Theo, you go ahead immediately, take some manpower, activate the defences, maximum radius, and implement the erasure programme – we're about to retire. Before you go, tee up a chopper for me, it'll be eight this evening before I'm ready, say eight thirty, prompt, from the rooftop here.

"Larry, arrange to rendezvous with the others in the morning, but between now and then spend some time in the office, delete the audit trails and shut things down."

The Password

Cape Town

When Rosy rang, later that afternoon, I was sipping an espresso coffee and listening to a busker playing his dented saxophone.

"Hi, Rosy."

"Where are you?"

"St George's Mall. I've got forty minutes to kill."

"The sax is playing Emavungweni."

"Beautiful, isn't it? Where are you?"

"I hate to say. I'm having lunch with guess who?"

"Peter Lipscombe?"

"Yes. Is it over?"

"Absolutely. How was your morning?"

"Not good, they spotted us pretty early on. Have you got a pen and paper?"

"I have, just making some notes for the meeting."

"Write this down. The password begins JJ 35, and the user ID ends with 149. You're good at crosswords, work that out."

"How long have I got?"

"Let's say five o'clock."

"Don't be ridiculous. What's the next move?"

"Hack in and try a brute force decryption, Karl's lined up a stack of machines to run in parallel. Anyway, I'll go now, the food's arriving. Speak later."

∞

In a committee room along the corridor from Andrew Mopeli's office in the Parliament Buildings, Joshua Chios, as elegant as ever, was sitting next to General Colby, both scanning the room's occupants. The two looked down from a raised platform centred in front of an end wall and a large oil portrait of Cecil Rhodes. Joshua Chios responded to the General's request for him to introduce the briefing with a wide smile and a tug of each diamond-encrusted shirt cuff before rising to speak.

"Thank you, General Colby. Okay, although I work with the Justice Department, for the past two years I've been seconded to Andrew Mopeli's Ethics Committee. The

Justice Department has always supported the Ethics Committee and has on many occasions publicly acknowledged the positive social input gained from the process of reconciliation and forgiveness. However, the Justice Department, together with many members of the Government, has also urged that certain individuals be excluded from the amnesty process.

"However, from today, with the expiration of the period during which the Ethics Committee was authorised to accept admissions, there will be no future grants of amnesty. Consequently the Justice Department is now free to pursue individuals without fear of them successfully avoiding prosecution by applying for a statutory amnesty. And ironically, the last two people to offer admissions, Stefan Taylor and Moses Kimbo, gave evidence against the Justice Department's most wanted individual, Jordan Atwell.

"In short we are here to discuss how Jordan Atwell and a handful of his cronies can be brought to book, given that the opportunity for them to confess and be forgiven has now passed.

"Lastly, the Justice Department, together with the Government, decided this operation would be inappropriate for the police and have given full authority and responsibility to General Colby.

"We also have Tim Kitson of the Johannesburg Post, who has earned a place here by assisting the Justice Department in its pursuit of Atwell.

"Thank you. Now, let me hand back to General Colby for the briefing."

I was pleased to hear that I'd earned a place, and enjoying the opportunity of being a fly-on-the-wall. There were a lot of people in the small briefing room, most of whom were unknown to me.

General Colby rose and began speaking.

"Why is this operation inappropriate for the police? I'll tell you why, we are dealing with a virtual army. They've got as much to throw at us as we've got to throw at them, plus, in their case, a few chemical nasties. Phase one of this operation is to arrest this man, Jordan Atwell.

At which point the General turned to point at the

screen of an overhead projector.

"We're going to raid his villa in Constantia Nek and detain him. You all know Constantia Nek. It's rumoured that as many villains as ordinary people live there, so we hope Atwell's demise will mark the start of an ongoing clean up."

There was a click from the projector and a change of slide. What appeared was an aerial view of a wilderness. Those present simply stared, silently, unenlightened, but not me – an inscription in the bottom right corner of the picture produced a rush of adrenalin, it said Jungle Junction.

General Colby continued.

"Phase two is a little more demanding. You're looking at a satellite image of several hundred square miles of twelve-foot-high papyrus grass. Somewhere under that papyrus is an astonishingly well-camouflaged drug manufacturing plant, a facility we need to find and destroy. According to Stefan Taylor with whom I talked earlier, the location is Jungle Junction and there is a labyrinthine network of navigable channels that makes the exact location of the plant difficult to identify, although it provides an ideal habitat for twenty to thirty thousand crocodiles. You can enter the papyrus by boat from the upper reaches of the Zambezi, the route out for most of the narcotics, or you can abseil directly into the central area from a hovering chopper."

I raised a pencil-clutching hand in an effort to gain attention but General Colby decided to finish.

"According to the intelligence we've gathered, an area surrounding the manufacturing facility is heavily defended with automatic weaponry.

"Captain Vorster has the operational logistics for an assault."

"Sir, it will take forty-eight hours to mobilise men, organise equipment and get there, half a day to move in and consolidate. We could be operational and established there by Monday morning."

"Thank you. Did you have a question Mr. Kitson?"

"Not so much a question as an answer. I'm pretty certain I can give you the coordinates for Jungle Junction's chopper set down point, I just need to make a phone call."

"Seriously?"

"Yes."

"Okay, Mr. Kitson, go make your call."

I walked to the room's far corner for a little quietness, away from Cecil Rhodes portrait towards Hendrik Verwoerd, the principal architect of apartheid. I looked up at Verwoerd's portrait and recalled Tsafendas, a man who upset the notion that it's the messenger who gets killed. Tsafendas was born in Mozambique, Greek father, mulatto mother, and worked as a parliamentary messenger in South Africa. In 1966 he walked calmly between the benches in the house of assembly, approached Verwoerd, unchallenged, and with an incomprehensible ease, stepped forward and slid a knife between two of Verwoerd's ribs and on through his heart, stabbing him to death.

I took a seat and called Schwartz and explained what I was after. A few moments later Schwartz had retrieved his GPS from the instrument locker and was back on the line.

"Okay, Jungle Junction's drop zone, in degrees, minutes, seconds, yeah? 17, 35, 25 south, 25, 01, 49 east."

"That's great, Marty, thanks. I'll catch you later."

∞

"General Colby, I've got what you need. Apparently you can hover directly overhead and the facility is still invisible. These are the coordinates for the abseiling access point."

"So much for the efficacy of my intelligence boys. Tim, I've failed to persuade you against coming on this mission. It's extremely dangerous."

"Journalistically, and personally, I need to be there."

General Colby nodded confirmation and strolled off to thank Stefan and Moses for their help.

I sat staring at my notepad, distracted, wondering about all manner of things. My pencil produced a series of insignificant short lines alongside the eastern coordinates of Jungle Junction, and then I saw it – the last three digits were the same as those near the top of the page, those that

Rosy gave me earlier as part of Atwell's ID.

"Hi, it's Tim. Rosy, have you got the right time?"

"Four forty."

"Twenty minutes to go! Rosy are you sure 149 is part of the user ID and not the password?"

"Shit, what have I missed? Karl asked me the same question. What are you thinking?"

"That 149 is part of the password, which is an extraction from the coordinates of Jungle Junction, and that's abbreviated to JJ at the beginning."

"You can't possibly have worked that out!"

"I didn't, I just stumbled on it. Got a pen?"

"Go."

"It's JJ 3525, which are the minutes and seconds south, and 0149, the equivalent eastern coordinates. I'm pretty sure that's it, and it makes sense that Atwell would use a Jungle Junction connection."

∞

After being thanked by General Colby, Stefan and Moses walked off to find a beer. I collected a voice mail, disconcertingly from the Northern Province police. An Inspector Jafe wanted to speak with me as a matter of urgency. I returned the call with a justifiable apprehension, and once connected sat silent.

"Your houseboy raised the alarm – he rang the adjoining farm and your neighbour called the police. The two dead bodies were in the lounge of your property. One victim was a semi-naked woman – looks pretty certain she was raped and then shot. The other was a semi-naked male who'd also been shot, but in an unbelievably frenzied way. The female was carrying a passport in the name of Emma Lennox."

"Oh God. Inspector, that was her maiden name. Emma married recently to Stefan Taylor."

"I'll tell you something, Mr. Kitson, the way her assailant was shot, well, mutilated, suggests that maybe his murderer was psychologically attached to the deceased woman – if her husband witnessed the rape, God knows. Have you any idea where we can find him?"

"It wasn't Stefan, Inspector. He's been here for the last forty-eight hours."

"Okay, I'll speak with my colleagues and get

someone to come break the news."

"Should I tell him?"

"Probably not, our people are trained in it and we need a statement. I'll get someone over immediately. The dead male carried a driving licence in the name of Gary Roper. Does that name mean anything to you?"

"Yes, yes it does."

After establishing my knowledge of the situation, Inspector Jafe offered his condolences and was gone, leaving me stunned. A loose tear fell from my cheek and smudged the Boss-man's password.

∞

"Mr. Kitson, Stefan Taylor has a working knowledge of Jungle Junction, can we get him to come with us?"

"General Colby, I've just heard that Stefan's wife has been murdered."

"Good God."

"Atwell's people are responsible. I'm sure Stefan will come along. Also, Marty Schwartz, he knows his way around the place, he's flown a chopper in and out of Jungle Junction many times."

"Good, get him too. So, we hit Constantia Nek in forty-five minutes."

"I'm ready."

Hooked & Off Again

Constantia Nek

After the clattering drama of storming Atwell's semi-fortified home in Constantia, Joshua Chios sat patiently while his team continued their work of search and recovery. I sat looking on, deep in thought as Atwell began speaking.

"Mr. Chios, you demanded I sit in this chair an hour ago. During that time your thugs have wrecked my house, and you have paced back and forth without a word of conversation and with a facial expression resembling that of a rabid Rottweiler. It is now a quarter past eight in the evening. I am on the verge of pissing my pants and I'm a little peckish. Perhaps you would like to tell me in your own charming way what the fucks going on.

"I'll tell you what's going on, Mr Atwell. I'm here to arrest you, and it's a total pleasure. First, General Colby has a few questions for you. By the way, we have not wrecked your house, we have searched it, thoroughly."

"And found nothing," Atwell said.

"Almost nothing."

"What do you mean?"

"We have your laptop's hard disc. In fact one of my team is booting it up as we speak, and he will shortly check out a little of your online history. I'm told there's not a question your laptop can't answer. I've been reliably informed it will assist me in the sequestration of your assets, the closure of your businesses, the identification of your co-conspirators and, importantly, the location of an amassed fortune in misappropriated funds."

My ears pricked up, almost violently. Misappropriated funds? Chios was after the money, Rosy's money.

"You can't just walk off with my Laptop."

"We haven't, we've taken the disc out."

"Or the fucking disc. You unfunny black bastard."

"Why not?"

"Kitson, you're a reporter, what are you going to

write about this farcical imitation of justice?" Atwell said.

"A piece that illustrates how a white supremacist exhibited his racist bigotry to the end."

"Fuck you too."

∞

"Atwell, you have an opportunity to co-operate, and it will be looked upon positively. I suggest you help us." General Corby said.

"And I suggest you stick your patronising offer up Andrew Mopeli's arse. It hasn't escaped my notice that you've raided me within hours of the Ethics Committee's closure. And Kitson, you fucker, you're in on this as well, seeing as you rang only yesterday to allay any fears I might have, and yet you pitch up tonight with the fucking army."

"Atwell, you have an opportunity to co-operate. I suggest you take it."

"Well, what I'd like to take is a piss. Look, Corby, if it's going to help, I'll co-operate. Listen, I need a piss, and there's a file upstairs that will interest you, I'll bring it down."

"What's in it?" Chios said.

"Operational info, distribution listings, other stuff."

I was startled. why had Atwell snapped so easily. He was offering up the very information needed for the morning, in order to save lives.

"Okay, go ahead. Private Brandon, keep him company." Chios said.

I looked on in disbelief.

∞

We didn't know at the time but Atwell had a prearranged chopper scheduled to collect him at eight thirty. So, when he rose from his seat with Private Brandon following him to the staircase, there were a couple of minutes to spare. After turning across the first-floor landing he moved to the second floor and out on to the roof garden.

"The information's in here."

Atwell pointed to a wooden chest, before bending to raise its lid. Private Brandon looked down but unexpectedly absorbed three bullets and fell to his knees, before seeing the handgun and its silencer that had just ended his life.

Atwell straightened himself and sped up the final steps to the helipad.

∞

Chios began shouted. "Jesus! That's a fucking chopper, overhead."

"GO. GO." General Colby shouted to the squad.

By the time the chopper skis contacted the helipad Atwell was already inside, pulling closed the door. The rotor blades pitched forward and the chopper was immediately obscured, falling into the safety of Constantia Nek's deep valley.

∞

"Sir, what the hell was all that commotion?"

"The bastard escaped in a chopper. What have you got from his laptop's hard disc?"

"A lot of very useful stuff, word files, contact files, spreadsheets, and the offshore bank details."

"Bloody hell. Where's the bank based?"

"British Virgin Islands."

"Well we can't do a thing until we've retaken Atwell and encouraged him to give us the password, which could be an enjoyable process if he refuses and I'm forced attach electrodes to his bollocks. Bastard. Stay at it, let me know if you find anything more."

"Sir, I already have more, a spyware scan was initiated on the laptop this morning, it discovered a Trojan. It's obvious somebody else is after the same information as us."

"Somebody else is after the money?"

"Yessir."

Brute Force

Lipscombes

"Tim has just given me what he thinks is Atwell's password."

"Really?" Karl said.

"Apparently he stumbled across it."

"You can't stumble across a password."

"I gave Tim the four characters we identified this morning and he recognised them, together with the characters I thought were the user ID. They're part of a location reference, map coordinates, for a place called Jungle Junction, which is the JJ bit at the beginning. According to Tim the password is JJ 35250149."

"That's remarkable. Rosy, that's also a particular type of behaviour, using a factual reference as the password. You can almost guarantee the user ID will be remembered in the same way, with a near factual reference."

∞

Peter Lipscombe walked towards Rosy and Karl and took a seat.

"How's it going?" He said.

"We think we've cracked the password!" Rosy said.

"So soon, how did you do that?"

"We didn't, Tim Kitson did. Actually, it was a complete fluke, Tim just happened to stumble across the original piece of information Atwell used to create his password – a map reference."

"Fantastic." Peter said.

"Peter, changing the subject, I looked through the listing of Fabio & Nicholson's personnel and didn't recognise a single name."

"Pass the printout. Let's see if I can recognise anyone."

∞

"Okay, the user ID, that's next. I'm pretty sure the user ID will have a similar aide-memoire." Karl said.

"God knows what." Rosy said.

"Brute force, that's what we need now. Let me

handle the set-up and get it going. Why don't you two take a break? I'll join you in a while." Karl said.

∞

"Thanks for the coffee, Rosy. Hey, you've told me your work involves the CIA, but not much else. What have you got in mind? I mean, why do you need two offshore accounts?"

"Peter, thanks for what you've done, and for trusting me. Listen, things have changed slightly. The CIA is no longer involved, and has handed over to Joshua Chios the pursuit of Jordan Atwell. Tim is after Atwell's story, and me, I'm after Atwell's money."

"You're worth a fortune already."

"Not for myself, for Amakhaya – the charity is structured as a trust foundation to provide monies for new homes. In the housing market the trust can act as a bridge between financial institutions and the poor, guaranteeing the repayment of loans, made to those who can afford them but are discriminated against, and giving straight grants to those who would never qualify for a loan.

"George Buckley did a similar thing, low profile though." Peter said.

"George Buckley, the billionaire philanthropist?"

"Yeah, his foundation initiated a scheme in partnership with the Government and the National Housing Agency. Is that where Dorothy Tutani works?"

"No, she runs the Azanian Housing Co-operative, very similar, though, and Dorothy and I are working together with Amakhaya – her political expertise coupled with my financial background."

"Why the offshore accounts?"

"I need the offshore accounts for moving money swiftly from the British Virgin Islands to Switzerland and then trickling it in here to avoid the Treasury's notification procedures."

"But you only need notify deposits over $500m."

"I know."

"You know! Jesus Christ, how much money are you talking about?"

"A few billion, compounded over a decade."

"Oh, fuck. God, to avoid notification on that it'll

take you months of trickling."

"Exactly, which is why I need to hold it offshore, once I've eased it out of the Virgin Islands."

"And why don't you want to notify the Government?"

"Well, you see, it's their money."

"It's their money!"

"Yes."

"Fucking hell! What has trusting you got me into? That's enough, okay, don't say another word. Fuck. I'll change the subject, so, how's Tim?"

"Pretty well, he's jealous of you though."

"Me?"

"I wind him up a bit, about us."

"He doesn't know you very well if he's jealous of me. He's the one you're nuts about, and always have been."

"I think you're right."

"Anyway, Tim's got quite a scoop right now, raiding Atwell tonight on the coattails of the military."

"Yes, they're presumably taking him down right now. Tim said he'd ring when it was all over, no communications allowed until after the assault on Jungle Junction."

∞

"Hi Karl. Up and running?" Peter said.

"The mass computer link's fine, the screen's an alphanumeric blur, characters scrolling down at the speed of light. I'll tell you something interesting, another computer has attached itself to the log in page."

"Who is it?"

"That's the interesting part, it's the Department of Justice."

"Jesus, and why would the Government be interested in what we're doing? I can't imagine, can you, Rosy? I'll see you both Monday morning, but give me a ring if you turn up anything over the weekend."

Sunday Evening

False Baai

Prior to the raid on Jungle Junction I was billeted with General Colby's soldiers, on the west bank of False Baai at the Swartkop army camp. The indigenous King Protea, the national flower, and chacma baboons, unique for living almost exclusively on seafood, surrounded the camp's perimeter. And although the sea lapped at the eastern edge and enhanced the camp's prettiness, it did little to ease my sadness at not having spoken with Rosy since Emma's death.

Through the tight-wired perimeter fence, in the shallows near to shore, a breaching whale opened its blowhole to propel water high into the air. I watched the fountain dissipate, imagining myself with Rosy in a boat on the bay, touching the whale, and each other.

I reached the officers' mess after flattening a few hundred daisies, uncharacteristically but deliberately scuffing them as I crossed the quadrangle, thinking of Emma, swearing under my breath. I went along to General Colby's update on the regiment's state of readiness, which was on schedule for deployment the following day. After the briefing we grabbed a coffee and strolled through to the lounge to catch the TV news.

"I talked with Stefan Taylor, before he left for Gravelotte this morning. He's agreed to trail blaze the boat boys for me, through the papyrus from the upper Zambezi. He'll be back in camp tomorrow morning. Said to tell you, Tim, he's spoken with Rosy."

"I felt awkward about that, not being able to talk with her." I said.

"Here comes the news." General Colby said.

We both watched a spinning globe appear on the TV screen, as did others involved in this story.

∞

"Listen up, Jabu." Moses said.

They watched the spinning globe fade and the news presenter appear.

"Tonight on the bureau's eleven o'clock bulletin, we

have a special report on the links between the Gravelotte murders, announced this afternoon by the Northern Territory police, and the sensational aerial escape last night of Jordan Atwell, one of the Justice Department's most wanted criminals. But first, with a round-up of the other main stories, Jacob Hatswa."

"The bastard escaped." Moses said.

The brothers eyed each other and took a gulp of their beers.

∞

Jordan Atwell, also watching TV, took a sip of his whisky.

"Fuck." Atwell said.

"What links?" Theo said.

"Search me, they can't really know. Can they? I thought Gillmor did a good job. Perhaps he fucked up."

"No, he did a good job. I've debriefed him, all was fine. And remember, Gillmor had quite a thing about Emma Lennox. It was hard on him, keeping his cool, but Smit's left the planet." Theo said.

"Then how did they link her death to me?"

"Jordan, there's a group out there now – Tim Kitson and the Kimbo brothers, and don't forget, Stefan Taylor is still alive and kicking, and maybe talking?"

"Taylor? You reckon? He has a good knowledge of this place. Expedite the evacuation, Monday morning, no later."

I D Isherwood

Lipscombes

Peter Lipscombe hadn't heard, he was too busy watching a quivering rod tip on the banks of the Orange River. It wasn't until he returned from his fishing trip that the news of Emma's death sprang at him from the newspapers sprawled across the back porch of his house. He read one front-page piece in its entirety before even stepping inside, and realised as he read it that Rosy, holed up all weekend, probably didn't know what had happened.

He decided that a telephone call was inappropriate and so, after a swift shower and a change of clothes, set off to talk with Rosy at the bank. Staff members working the night shift were surprised to see their chairman at such an hour, and they surreptitiously followed him in their peripheral vision as he strolled through the building to the IT suite.

"Peter, what are you doing here? I didn't expect you until the morning."

"No, I've come to talk with Rosy?"

"She's had a hard time this weekend. I don't know if you've heard, being away."

"About her sister?"

"Yes."

"I have, but I wasn't sure she had, that's why I've come down. How's she taking it?"

"Pretty well. Obviously upset, I think she'd like to talk with Tim Kitson but he's off somewhere with the assault force, incommunicado. Go have a word, I'm sure she'd appreciate it. You'll find her in the directors' lounge."

"Okay, I will. How's it going?"

"God, my heart's fluttered once or twice, when the interrogator flipped to ID verify, but then the verification failed. So, we're not there yet, but because we entered the password as known characters we're already sixty percent complete. And even if we have to go the whole hog we should be through by Tuesday evening."

"Fantastic, Karl."

∞

"Evening Mr. Lipscombe," the duty manager said.

Peter was retracing his steps through the IT suite towards the directors' lounge.

"Evening, Melanie. How are things?"

"Pretty much okay. It's unusual to see you here at this time of the day, sir."

"I popped into have a word with Karl, he's working on a special project this weekend."

"If you're looking for Rosy Lennox, she's in the lounge. Mr. Lipscombe, we have had a problem this weekend with the speed of the ATMs. I'm having it looked at, should be able to give you a diagnosis in the morning."

"Thanks, Melanie."

Peter walked on, thinking that a diagnosis of the ATM problem would be more appropriate for Wednesday morning, after Karl had stopped hijacking processing power.

Rosy was sprawled across a sofa with her head buried in a cushion, and even when he stood alongside her she was unaware of his presence.

When peter spoke her name Rosy was startled into a turn.

"Peter. Hi."

"I'm so sorry to hear about Emma."

"It's such shit, Peter."

"I've just seen a newspaper, it looked dreadful. How's Stefan? Have you spoken with him?"

"Stefan's beside himself, and he is so angry. He's pretty sure the people he knows from the army are responsible."

"You told me about that bastard Smit, from what I read at least he got what he deserved."

"True, but do you know what I've been thinking about? All the families that have felt the way I do now, thousands of them over the decades that Smit was out there murdering people, and hardly anybody said a word."

"You can't blame yourself for the actions of a maniac, or a murderous regime. You should have a clear conscience, and you're on the verge of doing something wonderful to mitigate some aspects of the past."

"Yeah, okay, I guess. Peter, something I've been thinking about is neither of us recognising any of the personnel at Fabio & Nicholson. We have a really wide knowledge of the banking world's people."

"I suppose so."

"And it says in their blurb that the security manager had hands-on experience with the seminal development of transaction security at Silvermans' Bank. Well he didn't, I ran that project with Karl as the techo, and neither of us has ever heard of the guy."

"What's his name?" Peter said.

"Isherwood."

"Nope, nor have I."

They walked back, but as they approached Karl's workstation Peter turned to Rosy.

"Something's nagging at me, but I'm not sure what. Let me have another look at that personnel listing, and Karl, take us online to Fabio & Nicholson's website. So this guy Isherwood, you've never heard of him but he's supposed to have worked with you, collaborated with you. Karl does their site have a section on key personnel?"

Peter was staring at Isherwood's name, with a total disinclination to look at anything other than Isherwood's name.

"No key personnel page," Karl said.

And then it emerged, the embedded mnemonic, illuminated, focused.

"Try security, and I'll bet the contact name ain't Isherwood."

"No," Karl said, "it's Daniel Peltier, the guy who worked with us on transaction security."

"Peter? What's happening?" Rosy said.

"This printout is Atwell's listing, from his machine. It's not from Fabio & Nicholson's website. Isherwood doesn't exist, he's Atwell's prompt. Look at his full name on the list."

"We are, you'll have to tell us." Karl said.

"Rosy, read it out, the full name."

"I D Isherwood." Rosy said.

They were both starring at Peter in the same glum

manner as Karl.

"Poor pronunciation. It should be is-her-wood, the ID is her wood. It may seem stupid but you have to remember this guy Isherwood doesn't exist. Try it out." Peter said.

"Okay." Karl said.

"Even if you're right, the ID can't be her wood. If it were, the word wouldn't be a prompt or a mnemonic, it would be the actual ID." Rosy said.

Karl entered the information and read from the screen.

"You have entered an invalid ID or password."

"Bollocks. Karl, I'm sure it's right, but maybe as Rosy says, not the actual word. Do you have a dictionary on your computer?"

"Yeah."

"Great, open it up and click on the definition search, and couple together, female and tree."

"There are times when I wonder about you, Peter."

"Rosy, in a moment you'll be grovelling in abject contrition. Karl, click search."

"Fantastic." Peter said.

He began reading the displayed computer matches.

"Box, Kermes, Service, Vesta. Only four. Okay, which one? Rosy, you first, choose a word."

"Peter, this is ridiculous. Okay, I'll have Vesta."

"Look it up in the dictionary Karl."

"Right, Vesta 1, a short friction match, usually of wood. That's the wood bit. Vesta 2, the Roman goddess of fire, in her temple a perpetual flame was tended by the vestal virgins. And that's the female bit." Peter said.

"I've always wondered what a vestal virgin was, you know, sixteen vestal virgins, that song, ah..." Karl said.

"A Whiter Shade of Pale." Rosy said.

"Try it as the ID." Peter said.

After a few moments Karl read from the screen.

"You have entered an invalid ID or password."

"Okay, Karl, choose." Peter said.

"I'll take Service."

"Service 1, a service tree. Service 2, of a male animal to mate with a female."

"Charming. I must remember that, very romantic,"

Rosy said.

"Try it Karl." Peter said.

And a moment later.

"You have entered an invalid ID or password." Karl said.

"I'll have Kermes," Peter said.

Karl enter the word and Rosy took a turn reading the definitions.

"Kermes 1, the dried bodies of female scale insects used as a red dye stuff. Kermes 2, a small evergreen Eurasian oak tree."

"Really very interesting." Peter said.

"Okay, type it in Karl." Rosy said.

"Oh my God! Welcome back Mr. Atwell." Karl said.

"Fantastic! Yes! Fuck!" The trio bellowed in simultaneous disunion.

Jungle Junction

The Army Declares War on Itself

I grimaced while the medic sprayed stinging merbromin along a deep gash to my right forearm, and a soft red cloud of anaesthetic and antiseptic settled over my skin.

"You'll be fine, and you're a lot luckier than some."

The medic nodded towards an injured soldier lying close to us, who heard the comment and became conversational.

"And I'm a lot luckier than some of the others."

"Next." The medic said.

I walked towards the injured soldier's bed.

"Luckier than some of the others?"

"The others that didn't make it."

"I'm reporting this assault on Jungle Junction for the Johannesburg Post. Do you want to tell me what happened?"

"Sure. After hitting the drop zone we were in and out of the water for a couple of hours, without incident, working our way through the papyrus in pairs, making safe. Schwartz and I were de-activating trip wires and de-mining as we moved."

"Schwartz? Marty Schwartz?"

"Yeah, the guy who led us in."

"Shit."

"Did you knew him?"

"Very well."

"I'm sorry, he shouldn't have died, he shouldn't even have been on the ground. General Colby told him to stay in the air, yet soon as the chopper stabilised he was out, first one down. It's ironic – he was so big, strong, made me feel safe."

I nodded, knowingly, stupidly thinking of the beer fridges we'd emptied together. I pulled out my notepad.

"What's your name, soldier?"

"Barney, Private Barney Enzo."

"I interrupted your story. Carry on."

"We had a sketchy sense of direction in that long grass, and we stopped to take a compass bearing. I'd just registered our track when a movement in the water caught my eye. Amazingly, I was on the croc before its snout even broke the surface. I moved to push Schwartz out of the way, a reflex, I suppose, but it was totally wrong. I should have just shot the fucking crocodile.

"I got a hand to Schwartz as he began to go over but the croc accelerated and twisted sideways, took him by the waist, but my arm was in the way and it got that first.

"It was fucking chaos.

"The water's not deep in those channels but the croc had us both under, and the fucker began shaking the air from our lungs. I can't tell you how strong it was, and the pain is hard to describe – teeth-puncturing pain, crushing pain, muscle-snapping pain. I kept my eyes open but it was hopeless. At one point a croc's head sped past, took Schwartz by the legs and began pulling. It wasn't until I tried to retrieve my arm and couldn't that I realised two of the fuckers had hold of us. The croc that had Schwartz by the legs pulled him away through the murkiness, leaving a stream of blood lingering in the water.

"And this happened." Private Enzo said.

The soldier took a pause and stared at his armless shoulder.

"Even though I was underwater I screamed. I was still held tight at the back of the croc's jaws. When it began spinning, Jesus. I felt my skin and muscles tightening without realising what was happening, and with each spin the pain got worse. On the fourth, I don't know, maybe the fifth turn, the pain ran into my shoulder and it exploded – my arm snapped off.

"And then, unexpectedly, I was floating free. I managed to clamber out of the water and call for help. I'm afraid it was too late for Schwartz, he was chewed through, bled to death."

"Fucking hell. Thanks, Barney, take it easy."

I pulled up a chair in what remained of the drug plant's refectory. I reinspected my sealed wound, intrigued by its colour, but also realising I was lucky. I arranged my notes on a trestle table and double-checked the chronology, with my thinking scattered amid flashing images of

Schwartz.

∞

Bruce Pontin had been waiting through the night for my call and answered the moment his phone rang.

"Tim?"

"Hi Bruce, are you ready?"

"Thank God you're alive. Yes, hang on, hang on, I'll get a pad. Tell me what's happening, before you file a story."

"What's happening is the story, and it's complete crap. There's easily ninety dead, mostly Atwell's men, including Theo Mason. Oh shit, Bruce, Stefan Taylor died, and Schwartz, Jesus, taken by a crocodile."

"Fuck!"

"On top of that, Joshua Chios, he's been interrogating, well, torturing, Atwell."

"Torturing?"

"Yeah, screams punctuated with blood-curdling shrieks, the unsubtle combination of electrodes and genitals. From Chios, just laughter.

"Fucking hell, for Christ's sake, Chios is a member of the Justice Department."

"Tell me about it! Bruce, another thing, a few of Atwell's men escaped, including Gillmor, slid into the papyrus with two or three others."

"Okay, that's enough. How are you?"

"I took a piece of shrapnel in the arm, mortar I think, apart from that I'm fine. Well, physically I'm fine; mentally it's mind blowing. Atwell's men were armed to the teeth and just didn't give a fuck. They couldn't even understand why people wanted them stopped. What's wrong with punching a few black lights out? If you're white it's all right, if you're brown stick around, and if you're black get back! Get back!

"Bruce, there's a bunch from Constantia Nek, Atwell's minders, eight or nine of them, they're ape-like, thick thighs, thick necks, shaven heads, tattoos and broken teeth. Even cuffed, they're regaling each other with stories of the African regimes they've toppled, the countries they've freed, which translates as the countries they've fucked.

"Anyway, Bruce, let's do it, try and run this tonight.

Tape machine on?"

"Is now, get reporting."

"In one of the oddest incidents so far in the country's post-apartheid history, the South African army last night declared war on itself. General Colby led crack units of the twenty-seventh regiment into combat against over one hundred of his own enlisted soldiers, all of whom, incredibly, were moonlighting as drug traffickers or mercenaries.

"The fact that the soldiers, elite Recce commandos, could exist in such a morally impermissible twilight zone, between the legitimacy of national defence and outright criminality on the other, will cause dismay within government circles and raise serious questions regarding the corrupt nature of the army's command structure.

"Some reports suggest that the covert nature of the soldiers' routine encouraged an autonomy that over time developed into a thoroughgoing anarchy.

"Apart from the shortcomings of the command structure a more pressing issue here this morning is how best to deal with the significant numbers of dead, estimated already to have exceeded ninety, and the many who are wounded and disorientated at having become casualties of their own army.

"How's it sounding, Bruce?"

"It's cooking!"

"Great! Okay, the assault on Jungle Junction, which lies deep in a remote papyrus wilderness, began towards midnight last night, when two Hercules aircraft of the 5th Airborne Division took to the skies over Cape Town with thirty Special Boat Squadron commandos. Having obtained prior clearance, both aircraft rendezvoused at Gaborone with four Chinooks of the 27th Regiment and flew on with them through Botswanan airspace to the Caprivi Strip.

"At around three thirty this morning, the boat squadron special forces were parachuted into a stretch of the upper Zambezi, where they deployed inflatables and began a push towards the criminals' camouflaged world, with the objective of taking out four surface-to-air missile installations en route, allowing the incoming Chinooks safe passage.

"Travelling with the boat squadron was a civilian volunteer, Stefan Taylor, an ex-commando with a working knowledge of the labyrinthine channels the boats were forced to navigate. Taylor's experience allowed him to lead the inflatables through the papyrus at speed for just over an hour, south of the Zambezi and north of the Okavango Delta and its swamps.

"The boat squadron's mission was a success, although one defence missile was launched, bringing down a Chinook. At this moment in time all fifty-plus soldiers and crew are either confirmed dead or are missing, presumed dead. The helicopter crashed with the most devastating explosion, sending an enormous boiling streak of redness high into the sky, violently rocking the helicopter in which I was travelling. The air around us became thick with the shadowy silhouettes of dismembered crocodiles moving upwards at strange angles, before swirling back to the ground."

"Jesus Christ!" Bruce said.

"The three remaining Chinooks blindly strafed acres of papyrus before hovering to drop their abseiling soldiers into the matrix of waterways that make up the Jungle Junction complex.

"Bruce, Colby's just walking past, hang on.

"General Colby, are you able to confirm the number of casualties in last night's operation?"

"Although we only lost eleven men in direct combat, an additional fifty-nine were killed when a Chinook, brought down by a surface-to-air missile, crashed inbound for the drop zone. Of those resisting our assault a further forty-seven lost their lives in combat. Also, and it's with great regret that I have to tell you this, both civilian volunteers have died. That's a total of one hundred and nine casualties."

"And how successful has the operation been?" I said.

"A complete success – Atwell, or the Boss-man, is now in custody and will face trial on a range of serious charges. Atwell's henchmen, with the exception of one escapee, are now also in custody or have perished during this engagement. The drug manufacturing facility is being destroyed as we speak and we have impounded a huge stockpile of narcotics. We have also seized an arsenal of stolen weaponry that Atwell and has been selling on the black market."

"General Colby, thank you."

I walked back to the table listening to Bruce.

"That was good. Tim, you said Schwartz was nabbed by a croc, but what happened to Stefan Taylor?"

"I talked with a sergeant Pik De Beers, here's an unedited piece based on what he told me – it's verbatim."

"Great, go."

"Stefan led us from the Upper Zambezi in open boats, banking corners at forty-five degrees, scattering egrets and barbel to the margins and keel contacting a croc every few minutes until we disembarked at Jungle Junction. It was misty around five this morning, but not cold, and we were crawling through the undergrowth and papyrus and stretches of tepid water. We came within a short distance of a hostile faction and could hear talking and occasional laughter, warning us of an imminent engagement. I was close in but Stefan was even closer, almost next to them and closing on their waves of chatter. I could see three soldiers standing in a small clearing, with an officer who was cracking jokes, and moving to and fro with a limp. All of a sudden the rattle of small arms fire took over, and string of cordite clouds rose from the papyrus. The soldiers thumped to the ground with a rhythmic randomness, and their groans rose in the laughter-less air. Amazingly, yet probably deliberately, the officer was untouched, but he stood in a rickety way among..."

"Stood in a what? You're breaking up." Bruce said.

"...rickety way, among the fallen soldiers, staring into the middle distance..."

"What?"

"...distance, seemingly waiting for a bullet of his own. And then Stefan Taylor stepped forward, pointing a..."

"Pointing a what? Tim?"

"Bollocks, lost the satellite." I said.

It was that part of the world, there's a hole in the coverage, lasts about three hours, so, back on again around four fifteen.

∞

It was a full three days before Jabu and Naomi laid their hands on a copy of the Johannesburg Post to read the full story sitting outside the nameless café.

"What's up?" Naomi said.

"Monday's Post, Tim Kitson is doing the writing and a lot of other people, including Stefan Taylor, are doing the dying."

"Stefan? Oh God, Emma, then Stefan."

"Listen to this. It's a first-hand account from a soldier Tim interviewed.

"Stefan Taylor stepped forward, pointing a revolver. On your knees, he shouted. But there was some hesitation from the officer, who we identified later as Theo Mason, and without a word Stefan put a bullet through Mason's thigh – I saw the back of his leg explode with the bullet's exit. He fell to his knees and Stefan shouted again, murdering bastard, something like that, and at that point the officer looked up and addressed Stefan by name, so they obviously knew one another.

"The officer said not to do it. He begged him not to do it, and to be honest I was shocked that he did do it. Stefan Taylor walked behind him and pushed the barrel of his revolver against the officer's head, nudged it forward slightly, so the officer was aware of the gun, and he pulled the trigger. The front of the officer's head exploded all over the place, and he fell forward into the mess.

"And then it was weird, almost immediately the wilderness returned to a strange silence. It was awful, and so was the realisation that I had a problem. As the officer in charge of our detachment I couldn't ignore what had happened, it was a summary execution, it was murder. I was slowly accepting I'd have to arrest Stefan Taylor when he pushed the gun barrel into his mouth and squeezed the trigger a second time."

"Aargh, shit! He didn't need to do that!" Naomi said.

Winner Takes All

Jozi

Rosy and Karl were on tenterhooks, waiting for Internet banking British Virgin Islands' style to start on a Monday morning.

"Karl, what time do you have?"

Rosy's inhalation of a fetid odour from her own body was rank, the result of having spent two unwashed days hacking and sofa snoozing, bereft of fresh air and soap.

"Fifteen minutes to go. It's eight forty-five in the British Virgin Islands."

"I can't believe it, the password and the user ID, just incredible. Are you nervous, Karl?"

"Yes, I'm nervous. I'm nervous because we're talking about mountains of cash, more dosh than the entire African Continent has spent on AIDS, ever. Yeah, I'm nervous. Rosy, there's a trickier dimension also, we're in a race."

"Yes, to get online, be the first to login."

"Jesus. I'm going to freshen up, back in five."

Jungle Junction

"Tim, what time do you have?"

"Three forty-five."

"Thanks." Joshua Chios said.

Joshua didn't realise he was in a race and so he was relaxed, reflecting on how enjoyable it had been extracting Atwell's password and user ID via his testicles.

"Joshua, what did you do with Atwell earlier? It sounded awful. Did you abuse him?"

"Of course not, I'm a member of the Justice Department. I was using a procedure that some might describe as shocking, but it's a technique Atwell is extremely familiar with, although he wouldn't normally be on the receiving end."

"Get what you wanted?"

And the answer came without words, a simple nodding confirmation with a smile of excessive self-satisfaction.

"What were you after?"

I watched an impeccably manicured index finger depress the laptop's power button, and before Joshua addressed the question he activated the laptop's modem and connected a satellite phone via Bluetooth.

"It's vaguely private, Mr. Kitson."

When I heard Joshua's response, several things occurred to me – the word private implied something personal, it was subtly different to confidential or secret, words more appropriate for government business. And Joshua had used my surname, a distancing ploy, less suitable for private matters.

"Joshua, when you say it's private, do you mean it's a personal matter?"

"Yes."

"So, the money that Atwell misappropriated, the fortune he has stashed in the British Virgin Islands, you're not attempting to reclaim it on behalf of the Government, you're attempting to reclaim it for yourself. Is that correct?"

"I don't know what you're talking about."

"The piece of folded paper, in your hand, it's radiating its contents to me."

"What contents? Wait a minute, wait a minute. Why has the connection failed?"

"The connection has failed because there's no satellite signal, and Joshua, there won't be one for another half an hour, until about four fifteen. I'm only guessing, but I think that's a little later than you would like.

"That piece of paper in your hand, it's shouting at me."

"Really? And what exactly is it shouting?"

"Let me see, ah, JJ 35, 250" I said.

At which point Joshua speedily unfurled the paper

in his hand

"Why don't you finish it off?"

"149." Joshua said.

He appeared confused, staring at the paper, exasperated, and beads of sweat raced to a dripping confluence on the underside of his soft oval shaped chin.

"Fuck you, Mr. Kitson." He growled.

Jozi

"Oh, that's better," Karl said.

"What's better?"

"You, you smell sweet."

"Instead of?"

"Doesn't matter, forget it. It's one minute to, let's go rob a bank."

"Right on, scriptkiddy"

"Here we go." Karl said.

In no time the login screen appeared. and Karl typed the password. Rosy felt her palms moisten, and she blew into the wetness to dry them.

"This is a joint venture, press enter." Karl said.

"Okay, the user ID." Rosy said.

Karl pronounced each letter with a clipping distinction as he hit the keyboard.

"K, E, R, M, E, and S."

He pressed enter. Their hearts were pounding.

"Account overview." Rosy said.

When the screen appeared they gasped, creating a rasping, whistling wheeze, both enveloped in a nervous energy.

"Karl, click transfers. OK. The account name is Amakhaya, sort code 303-40-13, account 01025863. Take it easy, okay, press enter."

"NO!" Karl said.

"What?"

"The amount, that's the longest number I ever saw! $3,582,176,374. Oh, shit.

"Ready? PRESS ENTER." Rosy was so ear-splittingly noisy other employees momentarily stopped work and peered over, intrigued to know what was happening. Rosy and Karl heard a loud click as the account overview screen disappeared to be replaced with a transaction message, which they read in conjoined silence.

9:07am Monday 19th January.
Your transfer request was completed successfully.
Thank you for using internet banking.
Would you like another service, Mr. Atwell?

"Press NO. LOG OFF. LOG OFF. KARL!"

Rosy screamed and flung her arms into the air and then around Karl's neck, with an uncoordinated jubilance that knocked them both to the floor, much to the amusement of others who intuitively knew to clap and whistle.

Jungle Junction

Joshua Chios continued mopping the rivulets of sweat from his forehead, and with an accomplished detachment, waiting for his mobile to hint at the satellite's return, and seemingly undeterred by my knowledge of Atwell's password. At nine thirteen his signal bar flickered to strength one and almost immediately jumped to strength five. There was a double-click of the computer's internet connection and a wait.

Joshua was considering my reflection in the screen of his laptop when Fabio & Nicholson's home page appeared.

"How long have you known about the money, Mr. Kitson?"

He keyed in the user ID and password extracted from Atwell's genitals.

"Joshua, get back to calling me Tim, it'll make our time together easier, more personal. The money, my father speculated about it years back, and recently the CIA confirmed its existence."

Joshua seemed exhilarated as the login screen accepted his input and displayed a welcome note, but the emotion was short lived.

Welcome back Mr. Atwell. 9:15am Monday 19th January
Your last visit was at 9:07am today.

Joshua clicked account overview. Three and a half years in pursuit, and the account balance was nil, all he could do was gawk in disbelief at the screen, and although the reality of the last transaction was obvious, at the same time it was unreal – the account had been emptied just eight minutes earlier. While Joshua gawked, I moved closer to gain a clear view of the screen. Unnoticed I smiled, Rosy and Karl would be beside themselves – they had snitched a financially gi-normous, monstrously large fortune from the baddies.

"Joshua, when you come to explain this, it will be impossible for the public to believe that you found the account empty. I mean, who else would have used torture to obtain the password. You stole the money, that will be the public perception, and the accusation, and what a great story – the new black elite, as corrupt as the white."

"Kitson, shut the fuck up."

Then in a heart stopping moment, Joshua pulled a gun from his pocket and pointed it in my direction.

"For fuck sake, put it down."

Joshua ended our conversation by squeezing the trigger of his chromium revolver. There was an enormous crack as the bullet shot through the laptop's hard disc, shattering it into a million mirrored pieces. Chios replaced his revolver, took hold of the laptop and hurled it over the twelve-foot papyrus into oblivion.

Recycling The Proceeds of Crime

Bophuthatswana

Dorothy Tutani spoke for thirty minutes at Amakhaya's fourth Annual General Meeting, held at The Solartropolis, a sponsored venue in Bophuthatswana, which enabled the charity's board of trustees to say a leisure-based thank you to their hundred and twelve staff – eighty-nine from the house building division, fifteen from the land acquisition office, six social and educational coordinators and two full time lobbyists.

"Rosy Lennox and I agreed to collaborate in forming Amakhaya, your housing charity.

"Was that a good decision?"

"YEEEEEES" the crowd roared.

"Rosy's input, expertise and fundraising abilities have been astonishing, four years of breathtaking financial wizardry.

"Where, you might ask, does she find the money?

"Rosy's skill has enabled Amakhaya to finance the construction of six hundred and twenty thousand new homes, rising from fifty thousand in the first year to two hundred and eighty thousand last year. Next year's build forecast is three hundred and twenty thousand. A million houses in five years!"

At which point the auditorium erupted, every member stood to either clap, whistle, stomp or scream. That included Daisy Ponbili, a worker and also a beneficiary of the charity's housing scheme. Daisy had stood at the lectern earlier to speak about her own experience of being helped by Amakhaya.

"I now have a home, in the new West Acre complex. I have my own space, to live in, to sleep in. I now have a toilet, a clothes line and a back yard. Before, in Soweto, I shared the back yard with a hundred and fifty people, the same people I smelt every day. In Soweto I lived with three million other people, here I live in a community of two thousand. The shanty huts of Soweto took my self-confidence as a deposit for somewhere to live, and my self-esteem as the rent – in Soweto I didn't belong. Now I do belong. I belong to the community, and I belong to myself."

The Courts Of (Rough) Justice

Pretoria

A few months after Amakhaya's annual meeting, on a Monday towards the end of September, and after one of the longest legal battles in the country's judicial history, Jordan Atwell was returned to the Courts of Justice in Pretoria for sentencing. Almost five years had passed since his arrest and trial, during which he was found guilty on a raft of separate charges, and finally he was to receive his comeuppance.

Joshua Chios was not in court that Monday morning. Almost a year earlier he had died of an AIDS related illness. General Colby was there, sitting towards the front of the court, behind the prosecution team's encampment. I was there with a bevy of other journalists, and we sat together in the press gallery overlooking the hustle and bustle below.

The courtroom was a stunning piece of Victorian craftsmanship, from the herringbone-patterned oak of the flooring to the Jacobean style wooden wall panelling. The raised seating for the judges was also a statement of intent from a time gone by, a time in which a wood carver could have spent a year sculpting the judicial bench and still have felt hurried, and behind the studded-leather seats of that bench a hand carved gold lacquered plaque blessed the country – Nkosi Sikelela iAfrica it said, God Bless Africa.

I counted eighteen rows of ornate courtroom seats, two of which were statutorily available to members of the public. The rows were swamped with a density of bums that defied belief, leaving us press gallery guys to look down over an assemblage of some two hundred or so judicial and governmental workers, together with members of the public and a scattering of armed police officers. There was a gale of chatter, colossal waves of intrigue swept from one end of the building to the other, blowing horizontally from the bench to the antechamber and its subway entrance, set off to one side of the public seating area, and from which

Atwell would in due course emerge.

"Please be upstanding." The Clerk of the Court said.

"The pre-eminent black judge, Senzo Manana, entered the courtroom with a palpable charisma and authority. As people seated themselves Manana nodded to his clerk, who in turn nodded to a warden standing alongside the subway entrance. It was an indication to bring Atwell through the sixty metres of subterranean corridor to stand in the dock, and there was immediately a recognizable sound of jangling leg irons as he began the journey. The sound was eerily amplified by the stark and non-absorbent acoustics of the white, gloss-painted tunnel, and in irons the sixty metres became a hundred and eighty echoing, shuffling jangles.

I asked the woman next to me who worked for Reuters what she was putting in her piece as a subtext.

"Given what's happened in this country, it's easy. I still can't believe Atwell collected HIV-infected blood and used it as a weapon. That has to be spelt out, clearly."

"His programme of maximum disruption." I said.

"Yeah, and how many people did he killed? He distributed infected blood over twenty years ago. He could be responsible for the entire epidemic."

I didn't have a reply. I simply nodded.

Suddenly, Atwell was there, standing quietly in the dock. Two police officers unlocked their respective handcuffs but not Atwell's leg irons, and motioned for him to climb the few steps to sit in the dock. For a second or two he didn't move, he surveyed the courtroom, allowing his gaze to settle briefly on certain individuals. He was barely five metres from the public seats, and the twenty or so faces that scrutinised his shackled body. It occurred to me that some members of the public staring at him may be relatives of his victims, come to see their day of justice. I thought it might even be true of the white male among them who had neglected to remove his sunhat, preferring somehow to remain anonymous.

Given the constraint of his leg irons, Atwell stepped sideways with a reasonable ease to take his seat, and when he turned to face Senzo Manana, the courtroom fell silent, but for less than a second.

"ATWELL."

The shout with its booming articulation was startling.

Atwell eyed the courtroom in search of the voice. Many others, equally puzzled, including me, joined a breathless wait for enlightenment. Yet for those seated near the voice, who flanked it in the public seating, where its face was partially obscured by a deep-brimmed sunhat, there was little confusion as to its origin, and as the voice stood, we all heard it again.

"A PRESENT FROM EMMA." Gillmor said.

At the same moment several armed police rose and bellowed across the courtroom.

"GUN! GUN!"

Yet it was too late for intervention. Gillmor, with a practiced accuracy and his commando's acuity, fired two bullets through Jordan Atwell's heart and a third into his head.

An armed police officer had Gillmor in his sights before the third bullet but safety compelled him to hold off, until the public had fallen out of the target's proximity. Without shouting a caution, in fear of Gillmor's next move, the police officer shot him dead.

Printed in Great Britain
by Amazon

51871250R00128